# Christmas Wedding

Serendipity, Indiana - Book Three

## By

*USA Today* Bestselling Author

## Magdalena Scott

Christmas Wedding

Copyright © 2015 Magdalena Scott

Edited by Karen Block

Trade Paperback Release: November 2015
ISBN-10:0-9862118-5-0
ISBN-13:978-0-9862118-5-0

Digital Release: October 2015
ISBN-10:0-9862118-4-2
ISBN-13:978-0-9862118-4-3

Cover Design by Calliope-Designs.com
Stock Art by www.thinkstockphotos.com

Jewel Box Books

# DEDICATION

For my favorite purveyors of marriage licenses

Shirley Batt
Melissa Burton
Vicki Dowling
Evelyn Hamilton
Sally Hattabaugh
Rita Martin
Beth Voyles
Susan Zollman

and Lois Gates ~ May she rest in peace.

Without the encouragement of these ladies,
Serendipity, Indiana, might not exist.

# DECEMBER FIRST

"So, what do you think, Mel? Is it time?"

I tore my gaze from the beautiful snow-covered Christmas trees all around us and looked at Jim. He winked then turned his attention back to his driving.

Had I missed something while in my reverie about work? My real estate office was doing well, but there was always something that needed my attention—and I wasn't doing any extras for work this month because of helping out in the evenings at the Standish Christmas Tree Farm.

I glanced at my six-year-old, Matthew, sitting between us on the truck's bench seat, but he didn't seem aware of whatever topic I had missed out on. He was mesmerized by the snow flurries we were driving into as the pickup made its way down the driveway and onto Tree Farm Road.

"Sorry. I must have missed something. Is it time for what, Jim?"

"You know. Getting married."

My heart immediately started to thump. "Married?" I whispered. "Now?"

Jim chuckled. "Not right this minute. We don't have a license for one thing."

"Aren't you forgetting something, Mr. Standish?"

"I don't think so. Bride, groom, license." He glanced down at Matthew and grinned. "Mini best man."

"Mr. Jim, the man has to be on the floor," Matthew told him then looked at me and smiled. "Right, Mommy?" It took me a moment to realize he was referring to seeing a man down on one knee to propose marriage.

"Exactly what I was thinking. You haven't been on the floor, Jim."

He chuckled good-naturedly. "Aha. Isn't that kind of old-fashioned?"

I relaxed, enjoying the topic as it became a bit lighter. "I don't care if it is old-fashioned. I've waited long enough for my proposal—a couple of years or a couple of decades, depending on how you want to count. Besides, I think we both deserve to look back on the traditional one-knee memory."

"I wanna see you do it, Mr. Jim. I only watched it on TV."

Jim groaned. At the intersection with Highway 56, he turned left toward our hometown of Serendipity. "Ganged up on again. I guess I should be getting used to it."

"Matthew and I are a package deal, so yeah, probably so."

"And what a package it is." Jim smiled and shook his head. "Very nice indeed," he said softly.

My face grew warm as I anticipated our goodnight kiss—a few stolen moments of togetherness.

When we turned onto North Main Street and my house came into sight, I sighed happily as I had done each time I approached it since moving here. If it hadn't been for the old Osborne place going up for sale, I might not have moved back to Serendipity after twenty years away. The big solid house had always inspired a feeling of strength and security in me when, as a kid, I had ridden past it on my bike. Later, on the night of our senior prom, the house had taken on a new importance in my life. A couple of years ago when I lost my real estate job in Fort Wayne, Indiana, I decided to buy a real estate business in Serendipity from a couple who were retiring. It had been an upheaval, especially for Matthew, for us to move two hundred miles south to the hilly, southern part of our state and my little hometown where I hoped I could give him a similar childhood to my own. Similar in location at least—but vastly better in other ways.

Jim pulled into my concrete drive that followed the north edge of my yard. He killed the engine. "Your Christmas decorations look great, Mel."

I had hired a teenager to help me string white lights all along the front of the house, outlining the shape of the big square home and also highlighting the deep front porch. The evergreen bushes by the porch wore nets of white lights. I had restrained myself from doing more, though it had been tempting. I know the kid was relieved to see the last box of lights emptied and also glad that we'd lucked onto a warmish day in late November to get the job done. The exterior lights turned on and off with the porch light, thanks to a helpful neighbor's ability with wiring. Tonight—December 1—was the first day I had switched them on, and I had been eager to do it as soon as I closed my office for the day.

"Mommy let me help do the candles in the windows," Matthew announced. "They're not real ones with fire. They plug in the wall." He sighed. "But they look pretty."

Jim patted Matthew's leg and opened the driver side door. "They sure do, pardner. Pretty like your mommy, right?"

"Yep. You gonna per-pose, Mr. Jim?" Matthew held his hand out to catch snowflakes, which were falling faster now. "You can come in the house if it's too cold out here."

Jim looked at me, and I nodded. I was surprised to feel nervous about it.

Key in hand, I headed to the side door, the way I always entered from the driveway, but Jim took my hand and tugged me gently toward the front porch. "C'mon, Mel. We'd just as well do this in full view of the folks of Serendipity." Matthew changed direction and trotted along beside us, adjusting his knit toboggan cap that Jim's mom had made him for Christmas last year.

Jim took me by the shoulders and positioned me on the front porch. "Okay. You stand right there. This house has been important to our past. Now it can be important to our future." He crossed his arms and looked at Matthew. "What do you think, Matthew? Should you stand by Mom or kneel down with me?"

"I don't know, Mr. Jim. I only ever saw a man and lady."

"Well, we need to make this work for us, Matthew. Hmm. I think you should stand next to your mom." Matthew climbed the two steps and stood next to me, and I took his hand. Jim knelt on the sidewalk at the foot of the steps and looked up at us.

"Melissa Mae Singer, I love you and I always have. Would you do me the honor of becoming my wife?"

My eyes filled with tears. "Yes, Jim. Gladly!"

Jim smiled up at me then turned toward Matthew. "Matthew James Singer, would you do me the honor of being my son?"

"Oh." Matthew looked from Jim to me. "Can I, Mommy?"

I squeezed his hand gently. "You sure can, sweetie."

"Okay. Sure, Mr. Jim!" He ran down the steps and into Jim's arms, nearly knocking him down. We laughed together as Jim stood and swept Matthew up into an embrace and gave him a noisy kiss on the cheek. Fluffy snowflakes landed on their shoulders, and I floated down the steps to my family.

Matthew patted Jim's face. "You did that real good, Mr. Jim. Did you practice?"

Jim mussed the little boy's hair and frowned to himself. "Once, a long time ago. This one was lots better in every possible way. And now that I've got it right, I'll never have to do it again."

I stood on tiptoe, one hand on Jim's arm and one on Matthew's back, and met Jim's lips for a tender kiss. There was hope in it, heartfelt promises, and at the edges, the passion we wouldn't be acting upon tonight.

When the kiss ended, Jim sighed heavily. "I don't like to see this day end, but I guess we have a first grader who needs his sleep. As does the most beautiful and efficient realtor in the county."

I laughed. "And a lawyer with impeccable taste." We all went up to the front door, and I opened it with my key. "Good night then."

"Wait! You're married now. Mr. Jim is gonna sleep here, right?"

Jim patted Matthew's shoulder. "Sadly, pardner, it isn't quite that simple. That was just the proposal. We still need to have a wedding." Jim took my hand and kissed it lightly, waggling his eyebrows as he looked at me. "I don't suppose we could schedule half an hour tomorrow to meet at the county clerk's office and get our license, walk upstairs, and let the judge marry us?"

I shook my head. "No way, mister. I won't insist on a huge affair, but I want something more personal than that. Plus we need to have everybody there."

Jim gulped. "Everybody?"

I laughed and punched him on the arm. "Your family. Mine, if they're interested. And I always pictured Alice and Carla and Francie as my bridesmaids."

"Oh, please. Seriously?"

"As you said, Jim, we're only doing this once, and we should do it right so we can look back on the memories—and the pictures, of course—for years to come."

"Tuxes, fancy dresses, photographer, rent a big hall in Louisville—"

"No. The church and fellowship hall are fine." I hugged Jim. "We can talk about it tomorrow. Try not to have nightmares."

Jim staggered wildly to the door. "One minute you're fine and the next minute you see your whole life flash before your eyes, including a giant dollar sign."

I pointed at the door. "I promise not to break our respective banks. Out."

Matthew and I went upstairs. After he brushed his teeth and put on his flannel pjs, we spent a few minutes choosing books to read before I turned out the lights. I leaned back in the rocker, admiring the brightly decorated walls that I had redone with the help of Jim's sisters, Carla and Francie, and our friend Alice. Trucks of every color and description traversed the walls. The girls and I had painted this room shortly after Matthew and I moved in—one of the few changes needed to make the beautiful home ours. But now what? Would Jim live here with us or would we all live in his much smaller cabin on the tree farm? If we moved, where would my real estate office be located? I loved having it in the large room downstairs with a view of Main Street.

# DECEMBER SECOND

I stepped into Carla's shop, *Creations*, announced by the bell above the door. She emerged through the purple velvet curtains that led to the workroom.

"Hey, Mel. This is a nice surprise." Carla glanced at a mirror as she passed, quickly checking her perfect hair and makeup. "What's up?"

"Wedding," I whispered, though it would have been fun to shout.

"Yes!" She gave me a bone-crusher hug. "When's the happy day? How did he propose? Do Francie and Alice know? And Mom? What does Matthew say?" She took my left hand. "And where, may I ask, is the diamond?"

"That's a lot of questions. Let's see—he proposed on the front porch of my house under the Christmas lights, with the snow falling—"

"Oh, swoon. That's pretty romantic for my big brother."

"—you're the first to know outside of Jim and Matthew and me. And Matthew feels kind of responsible because he told Jim he had to propose on one knee." I smiled, remembering. "It was perfect. As to an engagement ring— there won't be one."

"What? That cheapskate. After the big rock David gave Emily, you'd think he would have some idea what's expected. And back in the day, the ring Jim gave Diana was—" She clapped a hand over her mouth.

I shook my head. "Carla. Jim and I have talked. Things are different at this age."

"Don't you 'at this age' me. I'm almost that age, and I flatly refuse to accept a less-than-perfect bridal experience. For myself or for you." She held up a hand to stop my response. "It's not as if you've worn out the carpet walking down the aisle, Mel. As it's your first trip and about twenty years late, I say let's do it up right."

I took her hand. "I'm sorry you'll be disappointed with some of our plans, but Jim and I have decided to do things our way. I'm here to talk bridal gown with you. That's why I thought you might need to know right away. Jim and I are going to tell Lillian after work and then let the others know. I imagine the entire first grade has heard it already though. Matthew is thrilled." I sighed. "I need to contact my family, for whatever difference it will make. We'll book the church and see a florist and a caterer. Eventually, we'll go to *The Jewelry Box* to choose our wedding bands. I'm sure we'll manage to get everything together."

Carla was pulling out fabric swatches. "And the date is when?"

"Christmas Day. I hope that's not a problem."

She stared at me, goggling. Her mouth moved but no sound came out.

"Carla?"

"I—you must be kidding me."

"No. Actually it was Matthew's suggestion. Christmas has been so important to us and to the whole family, so December 25th is the perfect day." I smiled. "Right?"

"Next Christmas, I hope?"

"This one."

She sank onto a white and gold antique chair, clutching the fabric samples to her chest. "That's less than a month."

"It's almost a month. Today's just the second. So—do you mean you won't have time to make me a dress?" My breath caught. "I understand, Carla. I'll get something off the rack at a shop in Louisville."

She stood up again. "You will do no such thing." She grabbed my hand and jerked me toward the workroom. "Get that coat off, and let's take some measurements. I swear, if this family could give me a break during the Christmas season, I'd probably pass out from the shock."

\*\*\*

That evening, Jim and I held hands as we walked into the Christmas shop. Matthew followed behind silently, afraid he would blurt out the news to Lillian that he'd been telling his friends at school all day. As the mom of two of my best friends when I was a kid, Lillian had been a surrogate mother to me. What Jim and I had been through hadn't been easy for her, I knew.

Lillian was ladling hot wassail for a customer. Once she had rung up that and their tree and other shop purchases, she leaned on the counter, smiling at us. "I hear the Standish family is adding two new members on Christmas Day."

Jim slapped his forehead. "Oh, my word. Where'd you hear that, Mom?"

"Several sources. You know Serendipity. Bad news travels fast, but during the Christmas season, good news is even faster." She took my hand and Jim's. "I'm thrilled."

"Do you think it's crazy to get married on Christmas Day?" I asked, looking around as more customers entered the shop.

"Honey, it's not crazy at all. I love the idea. What better day for you to marry a man who lives on a Christmas tree farm?" Her eyes misted. "Harry would have loved the idea of a Christmas wedding. You know, he never gave up thinking the two of you would find happiness together."

Matthew had walked around the counter and put his arms around Lillian's waist. She leaned down and kissed the top of his head. "Matthew, this will be a wonderful Christmas, won't it?"

He nodded emphatically. "Can I talk about it now? Mommy said I gotta be quiet for a minute."

"Yes, absolutely, we want you to talk about it. Why don't you and your mommy and Mr. Jim go tell Mr. David? He's just outside, I think."

As the customers arrived at the cash desk, we started to leave. I quickly leaned across the counter and kissed Lillian's cheek. "Thank you so much, Lillian. And thank you for telling us about Harry. I hope somehow he knows Jim and I are together again."

She teared up a bit and waved me away with a whispered, "I'm sure he does."

# DECEMBER THIRD

I poured coffee into both of our mugs and slid my antique cream and sugar set toward Emily Kincaid Standish. In the two years I'd known her, she had transformed from Matthew's pleasant but childish babysitter into the confident and loving wife of Jim's brother David. It had all started with a car wreck the first autumn Matthew and I lived in this house.

"I don't really want a big wedding. I know Jim is afraid I'll invite thousands, but that's not my plan. I'd like to have all the family here, but I realize that may not happen." My family was very complicated.

Emily pulled a pad of paper out of her handbag and eagerly clicked her pen. "I'll do whatever you need me to, Melissa."

"Oh honey, I appreciate that. I know you've got plenty going already without my drama on top of it."

"Not really. I'm busy, but not overloaded by any means. We're family, Melissa, or almost anyway. Seriously. Tell me what I can do to help."

"If you could help coordinate info with Francie, that would be amazing. I grew up wanting Carla, Francie, and

Alice to be my bridesmaids, and it's hard to give that up. I don't even know if Francie can get here."

Emily wrote in her big swirling script. "So don't give it up."

"Oh, but travel this time of year is brutal. And what about her dress and fittings? I'm not sure—"

Emily held up her hand to stop me. "You know what I've seen that's awesome? Bridesmaids choosing their own dresses within a color family or a variety of seasonal colors. Like they could all wear red or green since it's Christmas."

"But some reds clash with each other. Same with greens." I sighed and stared for a moment at the small, bright arrangement in the center of my kitchen table. "I know what. How about Francie wears red, Alice green, and Carla does gold? Would that work?"

Emily was writing. "Awesomesauce. I'll get with them and pass it on. I'll talk to Carla first since she's making your dress." Her pen paused. "Wow. I wonder if she'll make hers too… And Alice's? I'm sure they'll be glad to text pictures of potential dresses to each other, right?" She laughed. "Like, we couldn't stop them if we wanted to. And we'll do the same colors in the flowers. Now, table decorations at the reception? What do you want there?"

Another item I hadn't thought of yet. I couldn't stifle the groan. "Oh, Emily. This is crazy. Why am I trying to throw a wedding together in less than a month?"

"Because you want to get married on Christmas Day. We can do this. I sort of have a handle on the process since I just went through it myself a few months ago." She smiled and blushed. "Of course, even if we make it simple, we want it to look good in the pictures." She reached for a cookie.

Oh boy. Pictures. Anticipating her next question, I shook my head. "No, I haven't gotten a photographer yet. Please write that down. Once we get the list made, I'll take it into the office and copy it for myself." I didn't expect December to be a busy month of real estate showings or sales, but mine was a one-person business still getting established. I couldn't close down to concentrate on wedding prep.

"Okay, Melissa. If you want to take care of some of these tasks, that's fine. I'll be glad to do a lot of it."

I was thankful for her words as I looked again at the lengthening list. Emily's and David's wedding had been anticipated and planned carefully for months and had gone off without a hitch. Emily had been a beautiful bride, and David was—then and now—obviously amazed at his good fortune. It was the stuff of which fairy tales are comprised.

In comparison, could I even get a photographer who would want to work on Christmas Day?

.

# DECEMBER FOURTH

We arrived at Lillian's that Saturday morning too early for Christmas tree customers, but just in time to meet the weekend's cabin renters. Two young couples were seated at the big dining table, enjoying a breakfast quiche and fruit salad. On the sideboard sat grapefruit juice and orange juice in large cut-glass pitchers, coffee in a silver pot, and a silver sugar and creamer. Lillian used her good dishes for the B&B customers.

"Well. This is a nice surprise. Susan and Tom, Sandra and Jordan, this is my son Jim, his fiancée Melissa, and Matthew." She motioned to us. "Children, there's plenty if you want to join us for breakfast."

"Yummy!" Matthew immediately scooted into a chair. "Is there cookies?"

"Are there cookies," I corrected. "But not for breakfast, sweetie. Not even at Miss Lillian's."

"Sometimes we have cookies for breffus, right, Miss Lillian?"

She dimpled. "Maybe once in a while." Lillian Standish is, hands down, the best chocolate chip cookie baker in the county, and the rest of her cookies are hard to beat too.

One of the men—Jordan or Tom—carefully set down his china teacup on its delicate saucer. "Mrs. Standish was just telling us a little about the town of Serendipity. We're going in to do some shopping after breakfast. This is such a unique concept—having your B&B in individual cabins and serving breakfast here in your own family's dining room. And all the extras make it even more ideal."

His companion—Susan or Sandra—nodded. "Really. I love the little Christmas tree in our cabin. It's darling! The whole tiny cabin is so cute! We're going to tell all our friends about it, aren't we, honey?"

The man next to her, whoever he was, nodded vigorously. "Very unique, and as my wife said, we love all the unexpected extras." He patted his stomach. "And the food is amazing." His companions agreed loudly. Soon all four rose and bid us farewell.

Jim and I automatically started clearing the table. "Mom, what extras are they talking about?"

She shrugged. "Oh, you know. Between Emily and myself, we manage to handle the Christmas shop and the little cabins without any problem. So it's fun to do special things people aren't expecting. Sometimes it's a wrapped cookie on each pillow with a little quotation about Christmas trees or solitude. We cut those little trees and add simple decorations, put them in the cabins. Hmm…let's see, between the two of us, we've come up with lots of fun things for our customers. It's nice to hear them say they appreciate it and are going to tell their friends. Word of mouth is the best advertising, I understand."

Jim watched her carefully, probably looking for signs that she was overloaded with responsibility since the B&B and Christmas season were both labor intensive. "You need more help with the B&B or at the shop? There are always people I can call."

She opened the dishwasher and started to load it. "I'm doing fine, honey. Just busy with work—and now the excitement of your wonderful wedding. It makes the season even more special."

Lillian was in constant motion and seemed happy. During the Christmas season, we all knew the memory of her husband Harry was nearer than usual, since he'd loved everything about the season so much. Everyone missed Harry, and we always would. He had died of a heart attack out among the trees, a couple of years ago, doing the work that not only made his heart sing but brought joy to hundreds of people each Christmas.

"When I finish here," Lillian continued, "I'll go out and see if Emily needs help in the shop." She finished loading the dishwasher, added detergent, and turned it on. Then she straightened. "Oh—did you need something? Or did you just stop by to eat?"

"We didn't eat anything, Miss Lillian." Matthew was eyeing the cookie jar. Lillian removed the lid and held it down to his level. He carefully took one without touching the others, and watching her expression, took another, his smile widening.

Jim took one too, barely fitting his big paw into the jar. "Mom, there's no problem if you want us to find more help for you in the Christmas shop."

She shook her head. "Thank you, but we're fine for now. Tassia Campbell—you know, Alice's mother—has volunteered to help in the shop and starts today, since Carla has a deadline on a brand new creation. Melissa is with me every evening." She hugged me briefly. "Until she decides she's too consumed with wedding plans. And Emily is wonderful help—like having two extra people. All that youthful energy. Next year might be different entirely."

Jim frowned. "Oh—why?"

"Well, I wouldn't be surprised if this time next year David was on the verge of becoming a daddy."

"What? Did they say something?"

"Jim, honey, they don't even know it yet. We'll see. For now Emily has plenty of time and energy for the B&B, the Christmas shop, and her husband. Next year we'll see how her time is spread." She smiled. "Not a problem now nor then."

\*\*\*

We left Matthew with Lillian, and Jim headed to the tool area to make sure the saws were in good shape, maps were in abundance, and everything was ready for tonight's customers. Most days in December, the customers were plentiful, unless it snowed, then the farm really became a madhouse. By the week just prior to Christmas, there were fewer and fewer customers, but even on Christmas Eve, some trees were cut and sold.

We were busy in the shop, and I was grateful Tassia was such a quick learner. She was also a calming influence, which I'd sort of forgotten since I hadn't been around her much since coming back to Serendipity. But the evening outdoors had evidently been less calm. As Jim took Matthew and me home, I could tell he was exhausted.

"Jim, you don't have to make this trip each night. I'm glad to drive out and back. It's no big deal."

"It is a big deal to me, Mel. How else will I get to spend time with you this month? Between working all day and selling Christmas trees all evening, there's no time for the two of us—or the three of us."

"Are you gonna live in town after the wedding, Mr. Jim? We have two extra bedrooms."

"Gee, Matthew, that's really nice of you. But you and your mommy will come to live in my cabin after the wedding."

"Jim—"

17

"What about my truck room?"

"Jim, we need to talk about it later."

"There's not much time for later. Wedding's only a couple of weeks from now."

"Almost three weeks."

"But not quite. You *are* moving to the farm...right?"

Frowning, I tipped my head toward Matthew, and Jim seemed to understand the warning signal.

That night after I had read to Matthew and he was sleeping, I went downstairs to the dark living room, lit only by the white lights on my tree, and called Jim. As the phone rang, I rehearsed what I wanted to say.

"Jim, you know we've discussed not wanting to upset Matthew by changing his life drastically too quickly."

"Yeah. Which is why I haven't hurried you. I mean, it's been more than two years since you came back to Serendipity."

"I think that's been the right thing for him. He's settled in really well and has friends and your family is like his own."

"My family *is* his own."

"Yes. Right. But remember, he's used to this house, and having his own room...."

"He'll have his own room in the cabin. You know that. I built the house just the way we talked about when we were in high school. A bedroom for our son and one for our daughter."

"Small ones. And one is your office now."

"Well? We don't have a daughter. We'll work it out when the time comes. We could even build on if we need to. What's this really about, Mel? Are you telling me you don't want to get married after all?"

"No. No, I do want to get married. I just—it's happening so fast."

"Two years or twenty-two, depending on how you count. That's not exactly supersonic speed."

I had said something similar a couple of days ago, hadn't I?

"I don't know where I'd move my real estate office. And I'd have to sell this house that I love so much? Give up the pool in the back that everyone has enjoyed these last two summers and being able to walk downtown if I want? That's not fair. Why can't you move in with us? Think how handy it would be to your law firm."

"More handy than I want to be honest. I want to be close to Mom in case she needs me, and you know the tree farm takes a lot of my time. Mel, I understand my priorities, but I'm not sure I understand yours."

"Matthew is my first priority. I also have to think about my business."

"And where do I land on your list?" he asked. "Do I even make the top ten?"

# DECEMBER FIFTH

I answered the doorbell and there, of all people, stood Jared Barnett. The last time I saw Jared he was fleeing Serendipity, and nobody had been more relieved than I to see him go.

"Ah. I can tell from your reaction that you remember me," he said, looking sheepish. "I hope you won't shut the door in my face, Ms. Singer." He shifted from one foot to the other. "I know I deserve it, but I still hope you won't. Because I've come to apologize."

"Oh? Why is that?"

He shook his head. "We both know I behaved badly last time I was in Serendipity. I don't deserve forgiveness, but I'm here to ask for it anyway. Also, to ask your help as a realtor, if you're interested."

I sighed and stepped back, pulling the door open wider. "Come in, Mr. Barnett." I closed the door behind him.

"This is a beautiful home, Ms. Singer. I thought so before too. Big and open and not jammed full of furniture. I thought it might have changed in two years, but it hasn't. You haven't either."

"Oh, I have, actually." I led the way to my office and gestured toward a client chair, then went behind my desk. I remained standing so I felt more in charge of the situation.

He smiled—a different type of smile than I'd seen from him before when he was here. This one seemed more authentic. Today's smile also made me aware of how handsome the man was.

Goodness, that hadn't occurred to me at all before. Back then, when I first met Jared had been such a crazy time in my life. I was just beginning to get established and concerned about how Matthew was adjusting to his new surroundings and situation and struggling with my feelings for Jim. I sagged into my chair. My past sounded too much like my current life.

"Well, if you've changed, I don't see it." His eyes flicked from my face to my left hand, and then back to my face. "I trust business is good?"

If Barnett had succeeded in his plan two years ago, business might have been better, but I'd certainly not be engaged to Jim. "Business is fine, thank you."

He cleared his throat. "I'm here for a couple of reasons. First, as I said, to apologize. Ms. Singer, I was completely out-of-line representing to the Standish family that you were working with me toward the sale of their farm. I won't attempt to defend myself on that. I was simply wrong. I hope you can forgive me—if not now, then in time."

"Are you going to tell me why you did it?"

His face took on a haunted expression. "At the time I wasn't myself. My wife was ill and had been for quite some time. My work was suffering because I tried to concentrate on her welfare, and yet we needed my income." Looking near tears, he glanced away for a moment and when he met my eyes again, his features were more composed. "It doesn't excuse my behavior, but I hope it explains it somewhat."

He had put me into a very awkward situation with the Standish family. Fortunately, they had been ready to hear my side of it, and then other people in town chimed in about how Jared Barnett had been scheming.

"Yes. I'm so sorry about your wife." I searched his eyes and found only apologies and sorrow. "Well, that's behind us now. I forgive you, Mr. Barnett. I realize sometimes life pushes us into corners we can't see our way out of."

His mouth turned upward in a tentative smile. "Thank you. I've thought many times about you and about what happened here. How is your son?"

Ah yes. The best salesmen remember to ask about the family. "Matthew seems to be thriving in Serendipity."

"I'm glad to hear that. It brings up my other reason for visiting you. I'm looking for a house here.

"A house? An investment?"

"Every purchase is an investment, of course," he said, looking more in his element. "But I'm interested in buying a house to live in."

"Here? In Serendipity?"

He leaned back in his chair, chuckling. "Yes. You shouldn't act so surprised. It might make newcomers wonder if there's something wrong with your town."

Truth was there were seldom newcomers to Serendipity. Lots of young people left, and local folks moved from one part of town to another, and sometimes people came back, as I had, after living elsewhere. But actual never-lived-in-Serendipity-and-decided-to-move-here type clients? Um, nope. I smiled at him, opened the binder in which I kept all my current client notes and wrote his name at the top of a page.

"Well, you've taken me by surprise. What are you looking for in a home?"

He leaned forward. "Something in town, preferably, or at the fringe. Four bedrooms, three baths, at the least. Two car attached garage, pool, not too much yard. Big family room."

It wasn't surprising he'd not even mentioned a kitchen. I made checkmarks in the appropriate boxes of the form I had created. "Do you want a vintage home or something newer?"

"Oh, newer, absolutely. I'm not completely useless at home repairs, but it's not my favorite thing, and I don't have time for it. No offense, but though this place is beautiful, it's—what? A hundred years old?"

I nodded.

"Right. Not interested in something like that. Too many possible issues."

"Houses have issues. I prefer to call it 'character,' and it's one of the joys of ownership, Mr. Barnett."

He laughed. "Our new house will have enough characters inside it, so it won't need much character of its own. I have two children, you see."

"Oh."

"The house we're in now is where they've always lived, but it's also the house their mother died in. She died in our bed, the three of us and the hospice nurse with her." The haunted look had returned, and after a moment he cleared his throat. "For all our sakes, it's time to move. I know there will be a lot of adjustments in moving to a small town compared to a suburb of Indianapolis, but we need this. I've discussed it with them and told them about Serendipity. I'll be bringing them to see the town, but today they're in school and work brought me in this direction. Two birds, one stone. Quite honestly, with Christmas nearly upon us, I'm even more motivated."

"The holidays must be terribly difficult."

"Horrible, really. Patty made the holidays happen. She orchestrated decorations, hosted parties, did most of the gift shopping. Every holiday is hard, but Christmas is simply the worst. Every time I walk into the family room right now, I automatically glance at the bay window where the Christmas tree would be set up... From what I've read, it's pretty typical to struggle during holidays more than usual."

"Most wonderful time of the year, the song says. But it's the most difficult time for lots of people. Oh my. I'll do my very best to help you and your family, Mr. Barnett."

"Please. Jared."

"Okay. Jared. And I'm Melissa."

Something happened in that moment. An invisible wall between us was removed, and our relationship changed in a subtle manner from purely business to something slightly more personal. Nothing wrong with that, nothing inappropriate. Nothing that, say, Jim Standish should complain about. Of course, he could because he was Jim. He had a slight tendency toward jealousy, and an inclination to harbor a grudge.

I handed Jared the local real estate guide that our cooperative published monthly. "We do have a few properties you might be interested in." Flipping through another copy, I told him which pages they were on. He pulled out a pen and circled the ones I pointed out. "When would you like to see them?"

"Is now too soon?"

"Well. You are eager, aren't you?"

He smiled. "Yes. You could say that."

Which is how I happened to spend a pleasant couple of hours with Jared Barnett.

\*\*\*

"Melissa, thank you so much for your time." Jared pocketed the business card I handed him. "We'll try for ten on Saturday then."

I nodded. "If something comes up, just give me a call. I look forward to meeting your children."

He smiled one of those proud dad smiles. "Katie would balk at being called a child. Twelve years old going on thirty. Oh, how her mother must be laughing at my attempts to deal with all the trials we face. Miles is as introspective as Katie is outgoing. What a pair."

"As I said, I look forward to it. And how old is Miles?"

"Six. About the age of your Matthew, I guess."

"Yes. That's fun. Maybe we can get the two of them together."

"I'm counting on it. When we move to Serendipity, we're starting over, so it will be great to see some familiar faces. Friendly ones at that."

I sighed as he drove away. The afternoon had been nice because he recognized my competence at my job. Because of his career as a real estate developer, he understood what my work entailed. If Jared and his kids did move to Serendipity, maybe we would be good friends. Jared could relate to the challenges of raising a child as a single parent and trying to keep a career going at the same time. Much as I loved my friend Carla, she was single without kids. Francie was married with a college-age son. Alice was married, and in spite of trying, she and Dean were childless. Jim, much as I loved him, had only ever had Matthew in his life, and so far that had been part-time. But Jared Barnett understood.

\*\*\*

"Barnett? That low-life who told Mom you were working with him to get our family to sell the farm the first Christmas after Dad died?"

Someone had seen the man come out of my house/office and get into his memorable BMW. And that someone had quickly given Jim a call. *Small town gossip.*

"That's the same person, yes, but he—"

"He's got some nerve coming back to Serendipity. I can't believe you're helping him find a house to live in here."

"It's what I do, Jim. I help people find houses."

"Mel. I know what you do. I'm saying we don't want this guy here, right?"

He didn't understand. He said he did, but they were just empty words. "You're not letting me tell you the story, so I won't. I spent a while showing properties to Jared Barnett, and we'll leave it at that."

Jim grunted. "I hope he didn't see anything he liked." He raised his eyebrows. "I *really* hope he didn't." His innuendo was clear.

"I don't feel compelled to discuss it with you, beyond the fact that I am representing him, which is also none of your business."

Jim closed the small distance between us and pulled me into his arms. I lay my head on his shoulder and tried to relax. "Mel, I don't want to fight with you ever, and this Barnett guy has caused two disagreements between us so far. I understand he came to you, and you're going to help him because you're a realtor. Let's just say I'll be glad when that's over with and he's either moved in or, preferably, goes somewhere else to live. I've met him one time and that was plenty."

"Jim, he's not a bad person. Trust me. Without divulging anything he said to me which might be confidential, just please trust me that Jared Barnett's presence in Serendipity is not the beginning of the end for our little town. In fact, I have a feeling he might do us some good. You know, it's not as if we get a lot of new blood in Serendipity. Might be nice for us to get a little shaking up."

Jim kissed my forehead. "I'm shaken enough right now, trying to keep track of my law practice, sell Christmas trees every night, and endure pre-wedding jitters." He kissed my lips, gently at first, and then more deeply until I was lost in the physical sensations that slid warmly through my body.

We finally surfaced, and Jim whispered into my hair, "I hardly have a free moment to kiss my girl, and that is indeed a sad state of affairs. Whatever happens with Jared Barnett is off my radar. I hope you sell him the priciest place in the county and get a big fat commission. How's that for supportive?"

"Nice." I kissed his jaw, realizing it hadn't been easy for him to say those words. "Very nice." If the Barnett family moved to town, we'd deal with it.

Although Jim wasn't naturally an unreasonable person, he did have a hard time letting go of grudges. He still hadn't entirely forgiven his ex-wife Diana for what she had put him through. Plus Barnett had caused Lillian and the rest of the family some anguish with his tactics. I realized that my easy forgiveness of him didn't necessarily indicate that the Standish family or the rest of the people in town would do the same. I should let Jared Barnett know that he had some repair work to do on his reputation before he could be happy in our little community.

# DECEMBER SIXTH

The day was cold, with a hint of snow. Jim squeezed my hand through our gloves as we walked along. "Why can't we just do this simply, Mel?"

"Oh, Jim. You keep saying that. Do you really want to get married in the judge's office or courtroom?"

He nodded emphatically. "I don't know why that's not good enough. I spend plenty of time in those places, and they're not so bad."

I wrapped my arm around his. "I'm sure they're just fine, but that's not how I always pictured my wedding."

He sighed dramatically. "Women and their fancy weddings. No matter how much money you spend on it, the result is the same."

"Yes and no. My way, we have memories of family and friends gathered with us on our important day. We have beautiful photos to look at for the rest of our lives." *Note to self: Find a photographer.* "Your way, yes we're married but, at best, we have a quick photo shoot with a guy who is likely eager to get on with his real work. It's what, five minutes? I'd feel silly even carrying a bouquet for something like that."

"People do it all the time."

"But not us. Okay?" We walked into the little church where we were both members. The secretary greeted us, and then Reverend Bobby came out of his office and pulled me, and then Jim, into bear hugs.

"Hello and welcome, Melissa and Jim. My goodness, how exciting this is. Well, come on back to my office and we'll talk wedding."

\*\*\*

Reverend Bobby shifted in his squeaky desk chair and steepled his fingers. "Holiday weddings always seem like a good idea but, in reality, they're much more complicated than doing the deed on a normal day. Christmas is particularly difficult. Family and friends are busy with their own celebrations, aren't they? Do you really want to complicate their lives by scheduling your wedding for Christmas Day?" He smiled, shaking his head 'no.'

Jim cleared his throat. "Mel is dead set on Christmas Day. There's a lot of meaning in it for us and our family. We do understand it's a busy time for people, but we're going for it." I was thrilled to hear him say that. "Are you telling us you don't want to do the ceremony?" His voice had taken on an edge.

"If you don't, please know we'll understand." I spoke up, hoping to defuse the situation.

The pastor leaned further back in his chair, and it squeaked more loudly. "The Advent and Christmas season are exhausting for ministers. From Thanksgiving until Easter, there's not an extra hour in the day. Somehow, I'm supposed to make it all meaningful for my congregation, and never mind the fact that I have a wife and kids whose needs are pulling at me as well. I have two boys playing basketball this year, as if I have time to go to their games. Varsity and junior varsity, of course, so two different schedules."

Jim stood up. "No problem, Bobby. We'll find somebody else."

The desk chair flopped noisily into normal position. "Now, now. I don't want to turn you down. Are you *sure* you can't go with another date—say something in mid-May?"

Jim looked at me and I stood too, forcing a smile. "It's Christmas Day for us. But we understand your concerns."

Reverend Bobby covered his big round face with both hands. "Christmas Day, it is," he moaned. "What time?"

\*\*\*

"That was fun," Jim groaned as we strolled back to his truck.

"I didn't mean to push him into it. We could have found someone else." Maybe.

Jim shrugged. "We didn't push. He caved because that's what he does. The man is too kind to ever disappoint anyone. At least he seemed relieved that the wedding will be in the afternoon. And there wasn't anything else scheduled at the church that day."

Emily and I had scheduled the church and reception hall a couple of days ago when I made this appointment.

The one concession we'd had to make was to have the rehearsal two days before the wedding instead of the traditional night prior to the ceremony. Reverend Bobby was hosting the community Christmas Eve service, and whether he realized it or not, we did understand that the real meaning of Christmas wasn't a Standish-Singer wedding.

# DECEMBER SEVENTH

"Katie, this is Ms. Singer."

Katie Barnett held out her hand, looking as self-assured as a politician at a fundraiser. I knew I hadn't been so poised at twelve.

"Hi, Ms. Singer. How are you?" Katie was tall and slender with blue eyes and cascades of golden blond hair. I was immediately glad, yet again, not to be the mother of a girl. I'd be tempted to lock this one up until she got married. She was so lovely and would attract hordes of suitors.

"I'm great, thanks. It's wonderful to meet you."

"And this is my son, Miles," said Jared. I looked down at the boy who regarded me with blue eyes a couple of shades darker than his sister's. Thank the Lord, his hair was straight as a stick, not curly like a cupid's, because if it had been, that's just what he would have looked like. A deadly serious cupid. The little guy stuck out his hand, having been well instructed. I shook it.

"Miles. Your dad told me you're the same age as my son Matthew. Maybe you and he can be friends if you move to Serendipity."

Miles frowned more deeply. "That's a dumb name for a town."

"Matthew said something similar when we moved here. He loves it now though. Maybe you'll get used to the name as he did. Do you know what it means?"

"My dad said it means happy surprise." Miles said it in a perfect monotone.

"Yep. That's it!" I clapped my hands together. "Well, this is wonderful. We have a beautiful day to look at houses. And—I hadn't mentioned it before, but maybe we could start off with a trip to the bakery for something sweet."

"No thank you. Our mother didn't like for us to have stuff like that." Katie hitched up her tiny, lime-green shoulder bag.

Jared's eyes went skyward, and he sighed quietly.

So, evidently, this day would be less fun than I hoped. "Oh. Well, then. We can all pile into my SUV." I gestured toward the door. "Shall we?"

It truly was a beautiful day, though being December, it was cold. Finding childcare on Saturday mornings in Christmas tree season could be a challenge, but I had settled on Matthew spending the morning with Carla at her dress shop. Carla, though glad not to have her own children, had a wonderful way with Matthew. She had set up a desk for him with plenty of drawing paper, colored pencils, and crayons. I think she was trying to nudge him toward a career in design, but as far as I knew, he drew only trucks or family members and Lillian's wonderful dog, Daisy.

I drove the few blocks to the town square and pulled into an empty parking space near *Creations*. "I thought it would be good for you all to see our town square. We have some interesting stores, several offices...well, let's walk around it and you can see. Okay?" I'm reasonably sure I heard groans from the backseat from both Katie and Miles. Jared was riding shotgun and smiled weakly at me.

"Sounds good. Let's go, troops." He helped Miles out since the SUV sits high, but just like Matthew, Miles didn't like having the assistance.

"First off, I have to point out this shop. My friend Carla owns it. She designs clothes, especially dresses, and sells them literally all over the world. It's unique that Serendipity has this little storefront, but most of her business is from elsewhere."

"Oh, wow." Katie, as if in a trance, walked up to the big plate glass windows that were on either side of the entrance. "Can we go in?"

Jared shook his head. "Honey, we're here to look at houses."

I shot him a look. "And yet, if this is interesting, maybe it would be fun to pop in." If we could help win Katie over with the presence of a really cool store like *Creations*, who would suffer? Other than possibly Jared's bank account as she got older.

Katie led the way, and Jared took Miles's hand when he began to balk. "Hey, buddy, there might be a store you want to go into and Katie doesn't."

The bell over the door jingled, and Carla immediately appeared from the workroom beyond the velvet curtains. "Good morning. Hey, Mel." Carla smiled beautifully at all of us, but especially at Jared. She held out her hand to each of them in turn. "Hi. I'm Carla Standish."

They all introduced themselves. Miles was horribly bored, while Katie was immediately enthralled and started exploring the shop.

Carla frowned in concentration after the introductions were made. "Jared Barnett. Your name sounds familiar."

I was surprised nobody had filled her in on the whole story.

"Yes. Well, I was here a couple of years ago on business. I created a ruckus trying to encourage the Standish family to sell their tree farm. So, if that's your family, maybe you've heard my name taken in vain a few times." He smiled wryly. "I deserve it completely if that's the case."

Carla shot me a look. "Oh. That Jared Barnett."

Jared held up his hand as if to ward off an attack. "Old and unpleasant history, Ms. Standish. I've left it behind and hope you'll be able to as well. My reason for being here—our reason—is to find a house in Serendipity so my kids and I can move here. As poorly as I handled business last time I was here, your little town still worked its magic on me."

Katie groaned and turned toward us. "God, Dad. You're so dramatic. Don't forget to tell her that Mom died so she'll really feel sorry for us." She turned away again and moved toward the back corner of the shop.

Carla's face registered shock, but Jared smiled crookedly. "Sorry. Was I being dramatic?"

Carla smiled back at him. "It's okay. Drama helps fuel my business. Drama and ego—and deep pockets, of course. So you're looking to move here? That's kind of a big deal. Where do you live now?"

"Indy. I know it will be a big change in many ways, but that's what we need." He mussed his son's hair. "Don't we, Miles?" Miles nodded soberly.

Carla called Matthew and he came through the velvet curtains, clutching a crayon, and looking bothered. "I'm drawin' a truck, Miss Carla!"

"Of course you are, honey. But look who's here." He came over and let me give him a hug and endured the introductions.

"You look six," he said to Miles.

"Because I am six."

"Me too. Do you like trucks?"

"Yeah. Who doesn't?"

"I have some of mine here, and I'm making trucks on my drawing board. Do you like to draw and color?"

"Well...yeah, kinda." Miles sent a questioning look to Jared.

"We'll be here just a few minutes, but you can go back if it's okay with Miss Carla. Matthew, it's nice to meet you."

"Yep. Me too." Matthew and Miles were beyond the curtain in an instant.

"Can't say I blame Miles for being bored with this whole process." Jared watched Katie's slow thoughtful movement through the store.

Carla smiled toward the girl. "Sorry, everybody. I seem to have a customer back here." She joined Katie, and Jared shrugged.

"I'm glad Katie's found something in town of interest," said Jared. "I realize the move will be especially hard for her."

"It will be an adjustment for everybody. It has been for both Matthew and me, but coming back to Serendipity was the right choice. I hope you'll be able to look back and say the same thing. Of course, we need to find you a house first. Maybe I shouldn't have suggested this tour of the square."

"No, I think the tour's a great idea. Stopping in here is already a big plus for both of them. So…Carla is a daughter-in-law of the lady who owns the Christmas tree farm?"

"Daughter. Carla's single, not that you were asking."

A half grin appeared on his face. "No. I wasn't exactly asking, but thanks for the info just the same."

"One of her brothers is my fiancée, if that helps complicate things."

"Oh. The lawyer?"

"Yes. Jim. You met him when you were here before."

"I remember. His face was a deep shade of red, and there was a murderous glint in his eye when I finished talking to him. What's the saying—I have 'fences to mend' with him."

I touched his sleeve. "You have a lot of fences to mend in Serendipity, Jared. Your techniques last time are legendary. There's a black mark by your name, and it will always be there. Over time it will fade, as long as from here on out you do things honestly."

He winced. "Wow. Why didn't you warn me?"

"I am warning you, but I don't want to dissuade you from relocating here. I love Serendipity, and it can become an even better place with new people who have big ideas. You need to know we're very slow to embrace any type of change, but it is eventually possible. Sometimes."

"Got it. I guess I need to decide whether I'm up for another challenge, or whether I should find a different town."

"You know best. Shall we go ahead and tour the rest of the square, maybe just from the outside?"

Since Matthew and Miles had struck up a friendship so quickly, Jared invited Matthew to join us. Katie obviously hated to leave the dress shop.

Carla touched Katie's arm. "Hey, Katie, if you move here, maybe you can join my sewing class. I do one for teenage girls each winter starting in January. Everybody picks something they'd like to make, and we just go for it." She snatched a flyer about the class from the counter and handed it to the girl. "I hope things work out for you, honey. Come back and see me again, either way, okay?"

Katie nodded, smiling more openly than I'd seen her do up until then. Obviously, those two had bonded. Relief was evident on Jared's face as he watched the exchange. The rest of the tour of the square was mostly from the sidewalk. Law offices, banks, insurance agency, nail salon, hairdressers, an antiques store, Bible bookstore, jewelry store, etc., were noted by Jared and ignored by the kids, which now included Matthew. The boys chatted about the trucks that drove past, especially the diesel pickups that could belch black smoke. Katie endured, though she perked up a bit at the jewelry store window. We stopped in at the apothecary and chatted with the soda jerk and pharmacist. Even Katie liked the idea of a soda fountain, and Jared said perhaps they could stop in after we viewed houses.

"I'm surprised at how vital the square still is," Jared remarked as we climbed into my SUV again. "And I think it's a little unusual to have a pizza place and Mexican, Thai, and American restaurants within easy walking distance in such a small town. Maybe we can have a late lunch at one of them in a while."

"After the soda fountain. Okay, Dad?" Miles prompted.

# DECEMBER EIGHTH

Jim and I took a few minutes for ourselves the next evening after putting Matthew to bed.

"Mel, I hope you've given more thought to coming to live on the tree farm." Jim's face was flushed—a dead giveaway that he was trying not to become upset.

"I've given it a lot of thought, and I keep ending up with the same answer. This is home for Matthew and me. I don't want to make his world too crazy by moving right away. How about you move here for a while so we can all get adjusted to being a family?"

He started to pace my big living room. "That doesn't make sense. It will seem strange to Matthew for me not to live on the tree farm. He loves being there, after all. You know how attached he is to it. I think your reason isn't as much about him as it is about you."

"What in the world?"

"I think when it comes to this house, you're still a girl who got jilted after the senior prom."

I crossed my arms and glared at him. "I'm not sure you want to bring that up."

"You're kidding, right? Surely, we're over that by now. Isn't twenty years long enough for you to heal?"

"I'm healed. But that doesn't mean there's no scar."

"Mel, you're being ridiculous."

My breath caught in my chest. "Think what you will. My concern is for Matthew, and that won't change. He will always be my first priority, Jim. I thought you realized that."

His face was dark as gathering snow clouds. "I appreciate you're his mother, Mel. And you're a great mom. But I'm his father, and I want what's best for him too. In my opinion it's important for a child to grow up knowing his parents have a strong marriage. These days that's often not possible, but with us, it is. Let's make that happen for Matthew. Okay? Our relationship needs to be central, and Matthew will be the happier for it. That's how my parents raised us kids." He reached down a hand and touched my cheek. "I know your family wasn't like that, and I'm sorry."

I pushed his hand away and leaned further back into the sofa. "Changing the subject won't do any good. We were talking about houses."

"I wasn't. Not really. I was taking about homes. It's not quite the same, is it?"

"Then let's move on to discussing offices. I love having my office where I live. You could move your office here too and rent out your building on the square."

He smacked his forehead with a palm. "You want my clients coming here? Trust me, that wouldn't work out well."

"Oh, come on. It would be kind of cozy to have our offices in the same space."

"No. Absolutely not. Not only don't I want clients coming to my home, there's nowhere in this house that would work. I have a law library, a file room, a conference room, reception area, and my office, remember? Not on the same scale as your operation."

"Don't say my operation like it's something unsavory."

"I didn't. I just said it's smaller and can fit in the den where you've put it. That won't work for me. End of story."

He stalked out and slammed the front door, leaving me shaken and uncertain—and not only about the house.

# DECEMBER NINTH

Emily and I left *Flossie's Flowers*, and I drove across town and pulled into the city lot off High Street.

"Hey, Carla. We're here," she said into her cell, as I slung my bag onto my shoulder. I was exhausted and on the edge of anger.

Carla flung open the back door of her shop and hugged us each in turn as we entered. "Ladies, so good of you to drop by. Do you bring me news of glorious flower arrangements?"

"I ordered some," I muttered, walking through the back workroom into the spacious showroom.

"Melissa isn't really feeling it today," Emily explained. I caught her mouthing something to Carla.

So, okay. I was in a lousy mood. Isn't that sort of traditional for brides? If it isn't, it should be, in my opinion. Even with Emily's help, I had a huge job to do and not nearly enough time to get it accomplished. It almost made it worse that the timing had been my idea.

Carla pulled out a white, wrought iron chair at the round glass-top table that was tucked discreetly into the corner of the shop. Many a man had sat there bored to tears while his significant other was fitted for dresses. I sagged into the chair and barely checked the movement of slamming my bag onto the glass. I dropped it onto the floor beside me instead.

"Tell all, Mel. We're going to get you through this, honey."

I sat up a little straighter. "Oh, it's okay. Emily was there, so she can tell you. Flossie's ideas were great, and the flowers will be fabulous. A huge bouquet in front of the sanctuary in colors that will match the bridesmaids' dresses once we know what those colors are. All our bouquets will match. Boutonnières for the guys, once I know exactly how many guys. Jim hasn't decided yet, as far as I know." I sighed. "Extra candelabras. White aisle runner, of course. Another bouquet at the guest registry. After the ceremony and pictures, the two big ones will go downstairs. Smaller versions all along the guest tables, and the ones we all carry will go into special vases and decorate the head table."

"Great. Sounds like progress," Carla enthused.

"Jim's going to hate it. To me it doesn't sound over the top, but I know he'll think it's way too much."

Carla shook her head. "Jim will be okay with it, Mel, if it's what you want." She was his sister, so she ought to know, but I had a feeling she was wrong.

"He balks at every step, Carla. He asked me to marry him, but after that, it's been one negative thing after another. He keeps suggesting we get the license from the clerk and get married in the courtroom. One quick trip to the courthouse instead of all this fuss." A tiny, almost nonexistent part of me was tempted to chuck all the planning and do just that.

Carla snickered. "He's a man. Of course he balks at anything that is pretty or feminine, which is what this wedding will absolutely be. Can we think of a way to give it a masculine touch too?"

"Seriously? Like what?" Emily asked. She'd been so lucky, because David would have put on a meat-flavored tuxedo and walked through a river of alligators to marry her if she'd asked him to.

Carla considered. "Well, like a reading. Or he could write his vows. Jim is good with words."

"I don't see it," I muttered. Emily looked from Carla to me and back.

"Yeah. Neither do I, actually." Carla smoothed her perfect hair. "Let's all try to think what would make the wedding something Jim could get behind." She smiled broadly. "In the meantime, we'll have a first fitting for the gorgeous gown I'm creating for you."

\*\*\*

Emily and I left the shop a little while later. She was in a hurry to get home to fix supper for David before the Christmas shop started to get busy. I needed to pick up Matthew at the after-school program at the YMCA. I dropped Emily in front of my house to pick up her car and drove on to the Y. The whole time I had to make an effort to keep my eyes on the road, because I kept envisioning myself in the gown Carla was working on. It was going to be everything I'd dreamed of. I really would be Princess for the Day on December 25th.

# DECEMBER TENTH

That night at the tree farm Jim handed me one of the slick travel brochures he'd snagged at the AAA office in Clarksville. "Finally, a piece of this circus that I can get interested in," he said. "Honeymoon plans. Let's go someplace tropical."

A show of enthusiasm at last. "Do you have a passport?"

He frowned. "Oh. I keep meaning to do that, but no."

"What about Matthew?"

"Mel. You don't intend to take him on our honeymoon, do you? I hope we'll have lots of opportunities to take him on trips. I want to show him some of the great places in this country, at least. But not the honeymoon."

"I didn't mean that. I meant, who will he stay with?"

"Oh. Mom or maybe Emily and David." Jim straightened the sign that listed the varieties of trees and their different features. "Of course, once Christmas is over, David will be traveling for work all week and only home on weekends. Maybe Emily could keep Matthew during the week and Mom could on the weekend."

I nodded, because this was how I had imagined it too.

"Could you ask them, Jim?"

"Me? Why?"

"Because I'm sort of swamped with everything about the wedding. If you could do that, it would take a load off me."

"You don't have to do all this wedding stuff, Mel. I keep telling you that. Quick trip up the courthouse stairs and it's over." He winked at me.

My eye roll was partly unintentional. I wrote in the notebook that had become my constant companion then tucked it under my arm and slid the pen behind my ear. "Okay, you're arranging babysitting for Matthew." I sighed, relieved, and leaned against Jim, his big strong body a comfort against the cold. "So, where are we going that we won't need passports?"

David and Emily came into view from their house just then, hand in hand. Bliss was written all over their faces. They had survived the planning of a wedding, reception, and honeymoon. We surely would too.

"Hey there, lovebirds," David called. He and Emily shared a long kiss, and he smacked her gently on the rear. Smiling brilliantly, she waved to us and went into the Christmas shop to help Lillian.

Jim grinned. "Hey there, little brother. You want to keep a G-rated atmosphere for us, please? There may be children around."

"I'll bear that in mind. What are you discussing so seriously?"

"Honeymoon."

"Uh—Jim—that's supposed to be fun. You look downright ticked. Try smiling once in a while." David secured the top button of his jacket as a chill wind blew through. "So, where are you going?"

"We don't know," we answered in unison.

"Better be figuring it out. You've got, what—two weeks?"

Jim groaned. "Don't remind me."

"Just thought I should. Getting airline tickets this time of year should be interesting."

"Maybe we'll drive."

"Okay. Where did you say you're going?"

"I didn't."

"How many hours you willing to drive? Are you just looking for a room or a place where you can actually do some sightseeing?"

"Room," said Jim.

"Sightseeing," I said.

David shook his head. "I think I'll go sell a Christmas tree. I bet every customer here tonight knows what they want more than the two of you do."

We watched him amble away, gloved hands shoved in his pockets, and Jim uttered something derogatory. It was the way these "boys" treated each other—all in good humor. He turned to me. "Long-range weather forecast looks bad in this area. If you believe in those. I checked earlier."

A discussion of the weather—our conversations had become stiff and awkward. I felt, again, weary.

"I tell you what, Jim. Come up with a couple of options, and we can discuss them. There's no time to sit down and do a lot of searching online together." I pushed my hair out of my face, pulled a band out of my jeans pocket, and secured it into a ponytail. A truck pulled into the lot and a family of four spilled out of it. Two more vehicles were coming up the drive. "I need to get into the shop."

I squeezed his hand and walked away.

# DECEMBER ELEVENTH

"You won't believe this," Jim said when I answered my cell.

I sat down on the nearest chair, getting a clue from the tone of his voice. "I hope it's good news."

"No, it isn't. A case that I thought would settle at mediation today has blown apart instead. It's scheduled to go to trial on the nineteenth."

"So close to Christmas? That's crazy."

"No kidding it's crazy. The judge set aside four days for trial, but we all assumed the date wouldn't be needed. But, as I said, mediation didn't go well." He sighed into the phone. "I'm frustrated about this."

Frustrated didn't even begin to cover how I felt about it.

"I'll bet. So you'll have trial prep on top of regular work, on top of selling Christmas trees every evening. You'll be exhausted."

"Yeah. And cranky. Don't forget cranky."

"Believe me, I haven't." Jim's temper was short during a trial, because of the stress of trying to do the best for his clients and the unknown result. He was a big proponent of mediation, believing it was better if all sides could have a say in the outcome of a case instead of letting a judge or jury decide.

"Bench trial or jury?"

"Jury. And, of course, nobody's going to want to be on a jury the week before Christmas. It's a struggle to get a jury any time. People come up with very creative excuses to avoid serving. Oh, Mel, I can't believe this is happening to us. What a rotten break."

"We'll be okay, Jim. I'm assuming you still want to go ahead with the wedding?"

Silence.

"Well, sure. Don't you?" His voice was soft.

"Yes. Plans are starting to come together. It's going to be so wonderful, Jim. You'll really be glad we didn't sneak off to the judge's office." I hoped that would be the case.

He grunted. "I'll be up there in the courtroom anyway."

I saw Jim later at the tree farm, of course. Except in a pouring rain, there was always work to do at the tree farm each evening during the Christmas season. But now that the trial was bearing down on him, Jim would stay at his office as long as he could before going directly to the farm. Matthew and I would already be at the farm, helping Lillian in the Christmas shop by the time Jim arrived, tired and testy.

When Matthew heard Jim's voice outside the shop, he dashed out to greet him. I followed.

"Hey, pardner," Jim said gruffly, lifting him easily up in his arms.

"Hey, Mr. Jim. Mommy said we can't ride in your truck while you do the trial."

"Yep. I'm sorry about that, pardner. It always cheers me up to have you and your mom riding along with me. I have extra work at my office this month, like I'm sure she told you."

Matthew nodded solemnly, and a hint of a pouty lip showed.

"It's life, Matthew. I have to do my best at my job. You wouldn't want me not to do my best, would you?"

"No. But the tree farm is your job too, and Mommy and me and Miss Lillian. How can you do your best at so many jobs?"

Jim sighed, and his eyes found mine. "You and your mom and Miss Lillian are my family, not a job. Sometimes the family has to be really patient."

"I don't like that part about family then," Matthew announced, wiggling to get down.

"I don't much like it either, pardner." Jim mussed Matthew's hair after setting him on the gravel drive and greeted me with a brief hug and kiss.

"Man, you guys are confusing me." David had just returned from giving directions to a family who were setting out to find their ideal tree. "Jim doesn't want an actual wedding, but now that he has to work extra, he's all prickly that maybe some of the wedding festivities will be affected by the trial." He jerked a thumb toward his brother. "Somebody is hard to please."

Jim glared at him. "I am not. I am very even-tempered. My concern is for Mel."

David laughed. "Your concern is that you aren't getting your way. News flash, big brother. It's a wedding. Not only won't you get your way, you don't even *have* a way. The trial is your punishment for being a bad sport up until now. Remember, I have experience. I lived through the wedding Emily and her mom so skillfully planned. And I did it by nodding and saying 'yes' a lot when my Bridezilla was talking. In order to get through your wedding, that's all you need too, Jim. Keep your head down. Be agreeable. You're not allowed to be irritable because you have a jury trial the same month. The bright side is you'll be expected to do even less wedding preparation." He smiled and patted Jim's shoulder, but paled considerably when he saw his wife

Emily, the former Bridezilla, had heard every word he'd said.

Head held high, she preceded me into the Christmas shop, and I nudged Matthew in too before I closed the shop door.

"Men," Emily said, laughing once she was out of David's sight.

Lillian, who was running the cash register without knowledge of our conversation, nodded. "Yes indeed."

Matthew shrugged and plunked down at his desk behind the counter and took up where he had left off coloring a picture of a monster truck the day before.

"Was Jim this difficult when Diana was making plans for their wedding?"

Lillian shook her head. "Melissa, please don't go down that road. Comparison is always a way to feel dissatisfied and unhappy."

"So that means…"

"It means, dear, that I would rather not discuss Jim's first wedding. If you find Jim would like to do that, I'd be surprised. That is in the past, and in the best interest of both of you, it should stay there." She looked down at Matthew, gently touched his head. "In the best interest of all three of you."

I knew she was right and I didn't want to compare anything about our situation with the relationship Jim had with his first wife. And yet, for some destructive reason, right now I felt compelled to do just that.

# DECEMBER TWELFTH

I stepped into Jim's office and greeted Suzanne, his administrative assistant. She looked as exhausted and stressed as Jim had last night when he met me at my SUV after I got Matthew buckled in for the ride home.

"Mel, I know I'm not very pleasant to be around right now, but as far as I know it's only temporary," he'd said.

I had smiled up at him, knowing this wonderful man was being pulled in too many directions right now. As Matthew had suggested, Jim had a lot of jobs this month.

"Jim, I understand. Or at least I'm trying to. I'm not angry with you."

"Oh no? Well that's a surprise and a relief." He'd put an arm around my shoulders, and I had stepped into his embrace. For a few minutes the sounds of the busy season had faded—the music, the crunch of tires on gravel, the conversations of the last customer and our co-workers were hushed as I let myself feel completely at peace in the arms of the man I had loved for so many years.

Jim sighed—a sound that seemed to start in his very soul. Of course, he was tired and working too hard.

"Jim—"

"No," he whispered against my hair. "Let's just be here together for a minute. Your love gives me strength, Mel. It always has."

I was surprised Matthew didn't complain about being left in the car for several minutes. Maybe he sensed Jim and I needed this. My son's perception sometimes surprised me. I was constantly learning how to be a mom. And our status would soon change, going from a one-parent family of two to a three-person family with a mom and dad. For so long I had given up hope of that and had, instead, done my best as a single mom. It hadn't always been easy to raise Matthew on my own, but it had always been worthwhile. Now, I realized I wouldn't want it any other way. All those years ago when Jim and I were dating and even talking about a future together, I had been willing and eager to simply be his helpmate in the future Jim wanted for himself. After he broke off our relationship, I left Serendipity—forever, I'd thought—and had chosen my own path. College, career, child. With no family that cared enough to help, I had done it on my own. Because of that, I came to this moment a much stronger woman. A woman who could state her expectations, or from a point of calm strength, be forgiving and flexible.

Jim sighed again, kissed my forehead gently, and released his grip enough to look down into my eyes. "Oh, Mel. What a crazy month this is. We'll get through it though, right?"

I nodded, noticing his eyes were damp. "Absolutely, we will. Absolutely. We're too tough to let a little extra complication derail us. Plus, remember we have lots of help. Nobody in Serendipity goes through hard times alone, and nobody in the Standish family faces anything without loads of built-in backup. We've got this. As David said—"

Jim tried to cut me off.

"No, hear me out," I continued. "David was right that all you really have to do is show up for our wedding. Emily is amazing help, and Carla—well, she'll make sure our wedding is a feast for the eyes." I kissed him, long and slow. "So, you do your lawyer job and don't worry about me and my wedding plans. I'll be sure to include you when you're needed. Stag party if you want one, wedding and reception, and honeymoon. Don't forget that."

"Oh, you better know I haven't. But we still don't know where—"

"Don't worry. We love each other and, really, that's all that matters." I shot him a big, reassuring grin.

His answering smile was a bit sly. "Great! We can get the judge to marry us. Tomorrow work for you?"

I punched him lightly on the arm. "Don't start talking that nonsense again."

"Well, then how about tomorrow we get the license?"

Excitement bubbled up in me. "Yes, let's do. That will make it seem more real."

"Meet me at my office at noon? We'll get the license and then have lunch together at *Chez Gwendolyn*."

\*\*\*

Suzanne let Jim know I had arrived and waved me back to his office. "I'll lock the front door and go to lunch," she said, snatching up her purse for a hasty exit. Suzanne was a fabulous employee, and I knew Jim expected a great deal from her.

"I'll tell him, Suzanne. Enjoy."

Jim stood and stretched, then greeted me with a quick, light kiss.

His desk was covered with files of all thicknesses and colors and a folding table jammed into a corner was also covered. There was barely space to walk around in the small room. "Wow. I love what you'd done with the place," I teased.

"Yeah, I know it looks tacky, but this is what I have to do to get everything organized."

I surveyed the disaster again. "This is organized?"

"Yes," he said sharply.

I put my arms around his waist, hoping for another few minutes like we had shared the previous night. "Okay. It doesn't matter how it looks to me as long as it works for you."

"Hey, Mel, I'd love to stand here and hold you—or you know, do more than that." He checked his watch. "But I'm on a schedule. Let's get that license and grab some lunch, okay?"

Deflated, I nodded and preceded him to the back entrance. He locked it behind us, and we crossed the street to the beautiful county courthouse.

I might be less than impartial, but I think our big stone courthouse is the prettiest in the state. It was built in the late 1800s of Bedford limestone and resembles a castle. The detailed carvings above the entryways weren't obvious since they were of the same material, but if you took time to stop and notice, the workmanship was amazing. Fortunately, I was able to do that on some of my trips here for work. There certainly wasn't any time to appreciate architectural details on this visit.

In the large foyer, we paused briefly at the door on whose glass *Clerk of the Circuit Court* was painted. I swallowed, suddenly nervous. Jim opened the door and let me enter first. I'd been in the courthouse plenty of times but not this office. At least two phones were ringing, a fax was feeding into a printer tray, and the women who weren't answering phones were working at computers. Or doing both, simultaneously. Yet we were immediately greeted at the counter by a slender woman who'd left her desk the moment we stepped inside.

"Hey, Jim." She smiled at him, then me, appearing relaxed in spite of the din. "What can we help you with?"

Jim cleared his throat. "Marriage license, Isabel."

She nodded, obviously not surprised. "Great. Just step over here, please." She motioned us to another area and requested our IDs, then began clicking computer keys as we answered a barrage of questions. The application process took about ten minutes. Isabel printed the application, we checked our info, and both signed. She signed and slid that document to one side and signed another form and stamped it with a large, antique-looking seal.

"This is your marriage license," she explained. "The person who performs your ceremony will fill in the place it was done and the date, and then sign. You will also each sign." She showed us all the signature lines as she talked. "Then it needs to come back here ASAP so we can get your marriage recorded. Oh—and Melissa, when you sign, you will sign 'Melissa Singer' just as you did today. If you're going to change your last name, you'll need certified copies of the recorded marriage to take to the Social Security office and Bureau of Motor Vehicles and whatever insurance, et cetera. You can always get more copies here." She smiled again. "Any questions?"

We both shook our heads mutely. Jim paid her and we left, retracing our route through the big north doors and down the steps. I slid my hand into my purse and touched the envelope the license was in. It was definitely starting to feel more real.

# DECEMBER THIRTEENTH

I answered the office phone. "Ms. Singer, this is Jared Barnett. I have a favor to ask."

"Oh? How may I help?"

"The kids and I need a place to spend Christmas. Or actually, we need a place to spend the next three weeks. Staying in this house is eating at all of us. It can't be healthy. We're all miserable, and it needs to stop."

I felt for him, understanding the emotions a house can evoke.

"Your offer is on the table, but I still haven't heard the seller's response. I'm sorry to say it's very unlikely you can be in there by Christmas, even if they accepted your offer today." The ten-year-old house on the street near the YMCA seemed a perfect fit for the Barnett family's wish list, and I knew their hopes were high.

"I understand that. What I'm calling to ask is whether you think we could get one of those little cabins on the Standish farm. From what I've heard and the video tours on the Internet, they seem ideal for us. Maybe a little cramped, but taking long walks outdoors would be great therapy too."

"If you've looked online, you know the phone number."

"I'm afraid they won't be willing to let us stay because of what I did a couple of years ago." He seemed to be having a hard time letting go of the past. He and Jim had that in common.

"I'll talk to Lillian. There might not be any empty cabins now. I don't keep track of that and haven't heard whether they're all booked for the month." I shifted in my chair, uncomfortable with the situation he was putting me in. It was one thing to engage my services for a real estate transaction, but I was leery of serving as a mediator of sorts between Jared and various members of the Standish family. So far it had gone fine—more than fine, I sensed, with Carla—but we were all under an ever-increasing amount of stress due to Christmas tree season and the wedding.

"If she decides there's not an empty one because it's me, I guess I can't blame her." His voice cracked a little, and my resolve cracked with it. "Thanks, Melissa, for speaking with Mrs. Standish. It's driving me wild to see the kids continue to suffer." Obviously, not only the kids were suffering.

"I'll give you a call after I discuss it with her, Jared."

***

I drove out to the tree farm to talk to Lillian in person about the B&B. She greeted me at the door with obvious pleasure. "Melissa. What a lovely surprise."

Stepping back, she invited me into her cozy home. It was no surprise she had a pot of tea and cookies available. We sat at the dining table, and she pushed the plate of cookies closer so I wouldn't burn any calories reaching for one. Hoping I'd still fit into my wedding gown, I dropped a cube of sugar into my tea and added half and half.

"Lillian, I've been asked to find out if you have a cabin available. There's a family of three looking for a place to stay, now through the holidays."

Excusing herself, she retrieved the scheduling book from her office and returned quickly. "There are a couple of cabins not spoken for during that period. But a family of three might find our tiny cabins a bit too snug, don't you think?"

"He's looked at them online and seems determined the togetherness and drastic change of scene is just what they need. It's Jared Barnett, and he has a son and daughter." I paused, watching for Lillian's reaction, but she just nodded so I continued. "Christmas is a very hard time for them, I understand. Lots of painful memories."

"That poor family. Of course they must come and stay."

"You do remember Jared Barnett, right?"

"Certainly, I do."

"He was afraid they wouldn't be welcome because of…before."

"Oh, goodness. I've forgiven him for that. Life's too short to hold grudges." She paused. "Please have him call me so I get the exact dates of their stay."

I had expected this graceful reaction from Lillian and called Jared as soon as I was in my SUV. He was thrilled and said he would phone her immediately. How interesting it would be to have the Barnett family on the tree farm during the season. For the most part, I wasn't aware of B&B customers' presence, but the more involved I became with the Barnett family, the more I developed a soft spot for them and wanted to be certain they felt at home.

As a single parent, I could relate somewhat to Jared's situation yet couldn't imagine keeping a family afloat after such a tragic loss. He had to heal while also helping the kids with their own grief process.

Katie was a confident girl, but her pain and insecurities weren't far below the surface. At her age, I was living with parents who doted on my older brothers and barely tolerated me. Without the solid loving foundation given to me by Harry and Lillian Standish and my best girlfriends, I could easily have fallen in with the crowd at school that was into drugs and alcohol as "escapes" from their own troubles. Would Katie develop good, solid relationships in Serendipity and walk into her future with confidence?

And Miles. He looked so unhappy, it hurt to watch him. I longed for the day when his sweet face wore a smile more often than a frown and he could look at the world with eyes filled with little-boy wonder, not sadness.

I expected a stormy reaction from Jim when he heard the Barnetts were staying on the farm and hoped Lillian's forgiveness would help smooth the edges of his anger. Sure, Jared had been in the wrong before, but many, if not all of us, do things under extreme stress that we wouldn't do on an easy day. If Jim would take the time to empathize, he might be more open-minded.

# DECEMBER FOURTEENTH

Thank goodness for the friendly, helpful sales staff at *The Jewelry Box* on the town square, who didn't mind that Jim and I had polar-opposite ideas of what our rings would look like. They just listened patiently as we described what we had in mind, took trays of rings out of the sparkling glass cases, and let us look at them, try them on, and talk about why each one wasn't quite what we were looking for.

Jim wanted a heavy gold ring, while I liked silver. He decided he wanted to buy me an engagement ring, and I'm sure it would have been sufficiently opulent to please his sister Carla. But I didn't desire big, flashy stones. I definitely didn't want something that would remind him of the beautiful, expensive ring he'd bought his first wife, Diana.

The people at *The Jewelry Box* took our differences and our needs and, no doubt, also our history in stride. They didn't get in a hurry, become impatient, or try to sway us from what we had in mind.

Wouldn't it be nice if all people were like that?

Wouldn't it be nice if my fiancée were like that?

Sigh.

Jim got more and more wound up.

I laid a hand on his sleeve. "Jim, I have an errand. Would you come with me?"

He looked at me in frustration but must have noticed the plea in my eyes. "We'll be back," he said as we started toward the door. I put my arm through his when we were on the sidewalk, and we ambled along in step.

"I just needed some fresh air," I said.

"That's the errand? Fresh air?"

"Yes. Air for our lungs and to clear our heads. Are we going to argue about our rings, Jim?"

"No. Of course not. I assumed you'd want them to match though."

"Why?"

"Well. Because I thought that's how it's done."

*Because that's what you and Diana did.*

"If I am to wear a ring for the rest of my life, which is my plan, I want to enjoy looking at it every time I set eyes on it. I like silver or white gold. I don't want diamonds. I prefer sapphires. But if you want a gold ring, that's fine. That's great. I don't want you to look down at your ring finger for the next fifty years or so and wish you'd chosen something different." By this time, we were a block from the jewelry store, had wandered down the alley, and were behind the public library.

Jim drew me into his arms. "Mel, for the next fifty years or so, when I look at my ring finger the only thought in my head will be that I'm the luckiest man on earth. I don't care—not much anyway—what kind of metal the ring is. All I care about is that it is one of many reminders that we've been given this second chance. That we've given each other a second chance." He tucked hair behind my ears and kissed me. "It's a little cold here for making out. We should either walk the two blocks to your house or the two blocks to my office."

So we stole a few minutes at my house before returning to *The Jewelry Box*. According to their posted hours, they would be closing soon but they still didn't rush us. I chose a white gold ring channel-set with small sapphires. Jim chose a gold ring with white gold edges. They would be sized and ready for us in plenty of time for the wedding.

Mark one more item off the to-do list, and we'd managed it without breaking up. Plus we'd managed a few minutes of private time together, which was a major feat for us at this time of year. The interlude was much needed though. I was glad he'd suggested it.

## DECEMBER FIFTEENTH

Jared Barnett dragged his kids to the Christmas shop. Katie looked bored out of her skull, but Miles brightened when he saw Matthew. Immediately, Matthew invited him to come around the counter and join him at the truck-drawing station. I admired my son for being so open and accepting and hoped he wouldn't change drastically from that attitude as he aged.

"All settled in?" I asked Jared.

He shrugged. "Not much to it. The cabin is a neat little place. The close quarters makes us get out for fresh air, and when we're in, we've got togetherness."

Katie groaned.

"A bit too much togetherness?" I asked her.

"I didn't know anybody actually lived in something that small. It's like a doll house. I mean, it's cute and all, but no privacy."

"I keep telling her to think of it as an adventure, but I'm afraid it's coming across as punishment."

"There's nothing to do," Katie whined.

Lillian came up after finishing with a sale. "What do you enjoy, Katie?"

"She's an artist." Jared's pride showed.

"Oh, Dad!"

"Well, you are." Jared put an arm around her shoulders. "She takes after her mother in that."

"There's no place to even put art supplies in that cabin. If I had any with me."

"Excuse me a minute." I stepped away with my cell and called Carla. She sounded overtired. I knew she was busier than usual because of my dress, but she was interested in my suggestion. We hung up, and I rejoined the Barnetts. Lillian was waiting on another customer.

"Remember my friend Carla with the dress shop?"

Katie nodded, her eyes lighting up.

"She's working extra hours right now, partly because of a big project I dropped on her. She could use nimble fingers if you like to do handwork, Katie. No pressure, just a suggestion."

"I'd love to try it! Oh Dad, could I?"

Jared touched her turned-up nose. "Wow. My daughter has returned, and the evil witch has been banished. Sounds great to me."

I enjoyed watching this man with his kids and wished Jim could take the time to do the same. Forgiving him would be easier.

"Wonderful. If you take Katie up there tomorrow, Carla can explain what needs to be done."

"Great." Katie's eyes shone, and I took a chance and gave her a quick hug. She hugged me back, and I could feel the relief in her slender body. The poor girl, losing her mother at such a young age. Maybe she and Carla would do each other some good.

"Still no word on the Shelby Street house, I take it?"

"No. Sorry, Jared. It's not unreasonable, considering the busyness of the holiday season."

He nodded, his disappointment evident.

# DECEMBER SIXTEENTH

My first business call of the day was from the realtor representing the house Jared was interested in. The seller had a counterproposal, of course. It was a step, and not unexpected, but for Jared's sake, I was frustrated.

I let him know, and he promised to stop by my office after dropping Katie at Carla's shop. A short while later Jared and Miles sat solemnly in my office. We discussed the money difference between his offer and counterproposal.

"I'm sorry Melissa, but I think the sellers are still too high." He suggested a counter, and with a sinking feeling, I put it in writing for his signature.

"I'm afraid they won't go for this, Jared."

He shrugged. "So be it. I can't see paying as much as they're asking."

"The house is in a great location. Close to the Y and schools and right by the walking trail. It's such a nice neighborhood."

"Don't push, Melissa. I appreciate what you're saying, but we're talking about Serendipity, not a metropolitan area. I won't go higher."

I was sorry for the kids and also for myself. I'd love to cut this deal, get the Barnetts in a new home where they'd be happy, and earn a nice commission. Men are so shortsighted sometimes.

It sure didn't help when Jim dropped in unexpectedly.

"Oh," was all he said when he saw who was in my office. Without a doubt, he'd recognized Jared. I was certain he would have said more if Miles hadn't been present. Jared stood and held out his hand.

"Mr. Standish, right? I've gotten to know your lovely mother a little bit."

"Yeah, so I hear. And my lovely fiancée too. Some people forgive and forget easier than others do."

Jared's hand dropped to his side. "That's certainly true. How long do you usually hold onto a grudge, Standish?"

"Decades, sometimes."

"That's too bad. My family and I hope to move here if I can find the right house at the right price. I had hoped to leave the past where it belongs."

"Barnett, you've got some nerve coming back to Serendipity, let alone moving here. We don't need your kind."

"Jim!" I knew part of his anger was his stress over the trial that was about to start, but that was no excuse.

"Sorry. Shouldn't have said that in front of the boy." Miles was glaring at him, and I didn't blame him at all.

I put my arm through Jim's and guided him toward the kitchen where we could talk privately. "What's this about? I didn't know you were coming over."

"That's pretty obvious."

"What is that supposed to mean? Please, Jim, don't keep saying things you'll wish you hadn't."

"I haven't said anything I'm sorry for."

"Then stop while you think you're ahead. Go out the side door, and call me later. I'm trying to run a business here."

"Yeah. Well, I see where your priorities are." He slammed the side door as he left. I was glad for the blast of cold air that replaced him in the dining room and gulped in a deep breath as I returned to my office.

"So sorry about that."

Jared turned as I entered, concern in his eyes. "It's not your fault, Melissa. I guess I needed to know that not all the Standish clan has forgiven the past."

I slid into my chair, shaking slightly as I drew it up to the desk. "Evidently."

I knew I was in love with Jim, but that scene stayed with me the rest of the day—long after Jared and Miles had gone, after I'd talked with other clients, fixed a salad for a late lunch and eaten it, staring blindly out the kitchen window.

Less than two weeks until the wedding. Brides are supposed to be the unreasonable ones at this point, right? I'm guessing that information came straight from the grooms.

# DECEMBER SEVENTEENTH

Carla called me to come in for another fitting. While I was in the dressing room, I heard Katie's voice. I knew she was eager to see how I looked in the dress she was spending ages sewing fake pearls onto. The pre-teen was at the shop as much as her dad would allow.

"Katie's not a problem at all, Mel. I love having her here," Carla had confirmed on the phone earlier when I called, nervous I'd foisted an extra responsibility on her. "Sometimes it's—you know—kinda quiet here. Katie livens up the place with her energy, and she's great with a needle. I remember when my fingers were that nimble. I think."

Now, shaking with excitement, I shimmied into the gown but could only manage part of the long zipper. "Carla. Are you available for some help with this zipper?"

In a moment, she had stepped into the dressing room with me, her face pink with excitement but her eyes straight down. "I'm not going to look at it until you get out where we can really see if it's working for you." After sliding the zipper up, she exited again. I heard her call to Katie.

"Honey, would you please lock the door and put up the 'Back in 15 minutes' sign? We want to be sure of some uninterrupted time with our customer."

"Sure thing, Carla." Light steps to the door. "Okay. We're closed. I'm dying to see how Melissa's gown looks!" Quicker steps toward the dressing area.

Carla knocked on the dressing room door. "Come on out, Mel. Don't make us wait all day."

I had hurriedly pulled my hair up in a French knot, and tugged a few tendrils out around my face and neck. This was something like the do I intended to wear for the wedding. I walked out into the larger dressing area where mirrors lined the walls.

Carla's reaction was immediate. She covered her face with both hands, and I swear started to shed tears. "Oh honey, you look amazing."

"O-M-G!" exclaimed Katie. "Just like a real princess." She tipped her head. "You can barely see the light reflecting off the pearls."

Carla put her arm around the girl. "You're right. It's subtle, but what a difference it makes. Turn around, Mel."

I did and saw in the mirrored reflections that the back side of the dress had less shimmer.

"See what I mean, Katie? The difference here where the pearls haven't been added yet?"

Katie nodded enthusiastically. "What do you think about a few sequins? Would that be over the top?"

Carla put a finger to her chin. "Hmm. We had kind of ruled out sequins, hadn't we, Mel?"

"I—"

"But now I'm looking at it, I do think we could add a few, like Katie said. Not overkill, you know, just a little more bling in a subtle way."

Katie's face brightened suddenly. "You know what would be amazing? Sequins that match the bridesmaids' dresses. Just a...dusting, like when snow falls and it just starts to sparkle in the sun, but it's not covering the ground." She shook her head trying to phrase it better. "Almost like you wouldn't notice them if you didn't know they were there, but when the bridesmaids stand with her, I think it would be magical."

Carla looked from Katie to the dress and finally made eye contact with me. "Mel? It's your call, but I think our girl has an idea that will make a fabulous gown even better."

"But how can we be sure about Francie's dress?"

Carla walked to the workroom and was back quickly, holding a folded piece of golden fabric. "We know the exact shade of my dress, so we can match sequins to it. When Francie gets to town, she presents herself and her dress here before doing anything else. Alice—no problem, of course, since she's local. Easy-peasy."

"Sounds great if you're both convinced it's not more work than you want to do." I wondered, though, if it were that simple, because it seemed nothing so far had happened without complications. Carla was going above and beyond and looked exhausted. "Um. Carla, what about your dress? Do you have time to make it?"

She waved a hand cheerily. "Oh sure. I have a week, after all."

Katie observed us, her brows knit in concern. "I'll help however I can, Carla."

Carla winked at her. "I know you will, honey. I'm counting on you, and that's kind of a big deal from somebody who's never had an assistant."

Katie's pretty face broke into a big smile. "I couldn't have imagined being assistant to the best dress designer in the world. I wish my aunt had gotten her wedding gown from you, Carla. Hers was pretty but just from a store. It was a different kind of wedding too. It was at the Indianapolis Zoo in the dolphin house, and my dad did the service instead of a preacher. It's what my aunt wanted—she's my dad's sister. So he got some kind of license so he could do it.

Pretty funny to watch my dad be nervous, because out in public, he always seems like kind of a big deal. I think he was almost as nervous as the guy my aunt married. Of course, part of it was that my mother wasn't there with us. He didn't have anybody to fix his funny bow tie until my aunt did it for him." She sighed. "I miss Mom so much. It's been more than a year, but sometimes I wake up in the morning and think I smell pancakes cooking in the kitchen, like she used to do for us on Saturdays. That's one of the reasons Dad wants us to move here. He says that house has too many memories for all of us, that we need to be able to make new ones—happy ones—someplace else."

Carla's arms were around Katie by the time she started to cry.

# DECEMBER EIGHTEENTH

Francie would fly up from Florida a little earlier than her husband Brad and son Joseph. The guys would arrive in time for the wedding but not so soon that they'd be caught up in all the craziness. I found myself briefly envying them that.

I was relieved when Alice volunteered to pick up Francie at the Louisville airport. I wish I had time to go since I hadn't seen Alice much this month. The crazy thing—and you get this in small town life all the time—Alice worked for the lawyer on the other side of Jim's jury trial, so she'd been working extra hours lately too. She and her mom, Tassia, were making Alice's bridesmaid dress. It was only a week before Christmas, and as far as I could tell, we were all exhausted. I hadn't seen Jim since the day he'd dropped in at my office and behaved so unreasonably about Jared Barnett. We had talked on the phone each night at bedtime, as was our routine, and even though Jared was never mentioned, those calls had begun to feel stilted. The trial would start tomorrow.

When we arrived at the tree farm, Matthew ran ahead into the Christmas shop. I didn't see Jim or his truck and asked David about him.

"I told him to stay away, that he was sucking the cheer out of the season for the customers." David nodded toward the man who was helping a family tie down a tree on top of their car. "Dean Williams is great help and drama-free. Gives him something to do since Alice is all caught up in her work. I feel sorry for Jim, you know, and it's not his fault the mediation fell through. But it's better for him and the rest of us if he concentrates on lawyering right now." David lowered his voice. "I hope you're not thinking of giving up on him, Mel. This is just a rough patch. Only temporary."

I nodded. "I know that." I also knew I'd added a massive load by wanting a real wedding, and on Christmas Day. Wanting those things wasn't exactly unreasonable, but it was hard on Jim to juggle the stress of the trial on top of working at the tree farm in the busiest month of the year and whatever wedding worries he might have. And I meant what I'd said about him just showing up for it. "You might be able to help, David. Do you know the number of groomsmen and whether they've rented tuxes?"

His face was expressionless. "I'll have to get back with you on that, Mel. I will—I promise. Just need to tidy up a few details."

In other words, he knew nothing, and no tuxes had been rented. I took a long breath, filling the time when I might have said something abrupt. "Okay. If you don't mind, I'd appreciate it." I smiled at him and went into the Christmas shop, where Emily was cheerfully helping customers and Lillian was talking to Matthew about his newest drawing. When Emily finished and the space was devoid of customers for a moment, I told her about the conversation with David.

Smiling, she shook her head. "Isn't it almost impossible to believe that men are able to, at any point in their lives, function on their own? I'll help David, and we'll make sure the guys get to Franklin's to rent their tuxes. Maybe this isn't a busy season for tux rentals."

Fear hit my stomach, hard. "Maybe it is though. Maybe they won't be able to rent anything nice."

She struck an astonished pose. "Oh. You want *nice*?"

I tried to stifle a groan. "You know, I'm not asking for cummerbunds to match the girls' dresses. Black tuxes, and if possible they'll each remember to use the boutonnières we ordered at *Flossie's Flowers*. Gee, Emily, how hard is it, after all the work we've done?"

"It isn't hard at all, Melissa, but we've been enjoying the anticipation of a beautiful wedding. Guys—at least, our guys—don't think that way." She glanced aside. "Right, Lillian?" Emily's mother-in-law joined us, looking reluctant.

I appealed to her. "You're in the middle of it, Lillian. Tell me, am I expecting too much for Jim to have decided who the groomsmen are and ordered tuxes?"

Lillian's face became impassive. "Please don't ask me to express an opinion on something on which you and Jim don't agree. As you know, his idea was to have the judge marry you in street clothes. His only wish is to be married to you, Melissa, and to become even more the father to Matthew that they both deserve. The way this month has shaped up, it's about as complicated for Jim as it could be. The only part of it that is less stressful than usual is the farm, thanks to David. He's the one who called Dean and told Jim not to worry about tree sales. I can imagine he worded it somewhat differently for Jim, because they always enjoy poking at each other, but still."

Love and pride in her sons glowed in Lillian's eyes. I'd been wrong to put her on the spot, to assume she would agree with me. "Melissa, I understand you want a beautiful wedding, and that in a way, you feel you've waited decades for it. I can see you girls with the glow that goes along with wedding planning these days. I don't fault you for it, and I'm sure I'll enjoy every detail of your special day. But you see, I'm hopelessly old-fashioned. Harry and I were married in a minister's study on a Friday afternoon, and our honeymoon was an overnight trip out of town. Our wedding photo was taken by the minister's wife, and the flower arrangement in the background was from a funeral in the sanctuary the previous day." She smiled, remembering. "It didn't matter to us, you see. Harry and I loved each other, and I was the happiest bride in the world. That's my hope for you, Melissa. That along with the wonderful gown Carla and Katie are working on and having friends and family gathered together among the lovely decorations, I hope on your special day, the focus is that you and Jim love each other and you feel like the happiest bride in the world."

Her eyes were drawn to new customers entering the shop. "Oh. I said I wasn't going to express an opinion, didn't I?" She chuckled. "Well, the other part of it is that I will call my friend Judy at Franklin's and give her a heads-up about the tuxes. But this is absolutely the last time I will help either of my boys prepare for a wedding. I'm getting too old for this." Lillian sailed off to talk to the customers, and Emily and I stood for a moment, watching her.

"She's not too old for anything," I said.

Emily laughed. "The woman is made of energy. I've seen the wedding photo she was talking about. It's on the buffet with a lot of other family photos. It never occurred to me the flowers in the background weren't wedding flowers."

"I guess they were for that moment in time."

"Yeah. You do with what you have. Lucky us, to be able to order the perfect flowers and set up the church and reception hall just the way you want it. Oh, Melissa, your wedding will be so amazing. With the touches Flossie is putting on the bouquets and the gorgeous cake from *Something Sweet*, plus Carla and Katie's detail work on your gown, everybody will remember it for a long time. Plus you'll have awesome pictures." She paused, and we both imagined the event we were working toward. "So, all this talk of tuxes reminds me. Is Matthew going to wear one too?"

75

My stomach turned over. Who was I to fuss about Jim's lack of attention to the tuxes, when I had forgotten to take my own son in for measurements? It was on my to-do list— wherever that was.

# DECEMBER NINETEENTH

The minute she was off the plane, Francie shot me a text to let me know *Your imported bridesmaid has landed!*

It seemed to take forever for her and Alice to drive to Serendipity. When I got the text that they'd entered the city limits on their way to *Creations*, I put the closed sign on the front door, jumped into my SUV, and drove over there. Our group hug when they emerged from Alice's car was tearful but didn't last long.

Francie's teeth were already chattering. "Wow. This is brutal after leaving Florida with sun and seventy degree temps."

I put my arms through theirs, and her dress bag whipped in the wind as we hurried toward Carla's shop. "Your blood has thinned out again."

We burst through the front door laughing together, and I hurriedly shut it against the cold wind. Carla's face lit up as she embraced first her sister Francie then Alice in a long hug.

"I can't wait to see your wedding gown," Alice said. "It's almost surreal, after all these years." She nudged me. "Well, go put it on for us."

Francie giggled. "I haven't been able to sleep nights. Carla refused to send a picture of even part of it. How mean. So, tell me more about the girl helping with the detail work."

Carla put up her "Closed" sign, and I explained about Katie as we wended our way to the dressing area. "Well, Katie is really talented. I think Carla wonders how she could have done this without her. She's the daughter of Jared Barnett."

Francie's frown was immediate. "Right. Are you sure we can trust that guy? I mean, I understand the daughter is fine, but he was a real skunk."

I paused. "He's okay, Francie. Extenuating circumstances."

Carla explained about his wife's illness and her death since then and that the family was living in one of the little cabins on the tree farm while they waited for news about the house they wanted to buy.

Francie unzipped her dress bag which she'd hung on the wall in the larger dressing area with all the mirrors. "He's either a great dad or half crazy to live in one of those with two kids."

Carla had her back to us when she said, "A great dad, I think."

"And handsome on top of that. Right, Carla?" I watched in the mirror as her slight blush began its slow creep up her neck.

She cleared her throat, turned, and fussed to help me with my gown. "I'd say that's rather obvious."

"Right," Francie said softly, watching her with raised eyebrows. Alice looked from one sister to the other then focused on another dress bag I hadn't noticed before.

"Carla? Where's your dress?" Francie asked.

"It's in process. I'll have it ready in time, never fear."

"And you'll look amazing as always," I said as she secured my long zipper. I worked briefly on my hair as I'd done before. It was a couple of minutes before I realized all three were watching me.

"Oh my goodness. That is the most exquisite wedding gown ever!" Francie hugged Carla. "You are the best."

Alice delicately touched the skirt. "Wow. It really is, honey. Classic, yet one of a kind."

I looked at our reflections. All the dresses were tea length with slim bodices, long tapered sleeves, and full skirts. And they were all of satin. My white one had a portrait neckline, and the pearls and sequins. Francie's dress was the perfect shade of traditional Christmas red, Alice's holly green, both with V-necks. They were fabulous in their simplicity, unadorned by sequins or pearls. Carla slipped into the workroom and returned holding her partially-completed gold dress in front of her.

"Huddle up," she directed. The combination of the rich colors with mine—both in the mirrors and with bare eyes—was nearly breathtaking.

"Oh, girls, I couldn't have imagined anything prettier. How did you do it? Everybody used the same pattern?"

Francie nodded, smiling. "To state it simply, yes. There are places where you can get a dress custom made, even in a hurry. Of course those shops are not as good as our Carla, but I think it worked out. You're pleased, Mel?"

"Oh my. I love them all. Alice, who did you find to make yours?"

She smiled. "I had an excellent pattern, cut to fit thanks to Carla, and I am blessed with a very talented mother. I was in the process of making it myself until the jury trial reared its ugly head. I think our junior high home ec teacher would have been proud to see the results of her instruction."

Francie turned her back to Alice and gestured toward the zipper so Alice could undo her. "Thanks for not making us wear something godawful, Mel."

"Glad to oblige, for sure. Thank you for having such beautiful dresses made. And Carla. Where would we have been without our very own designer?"

Carla draped her dress-in-progress over a nearby chair. "Up a creek without a bolt of cloth to paddle with, my dear. I'll get mine done in a day or so. For some bizarre reason Christmas is a busy season for me. Don't people know I have other things to do?" Her smile was tired but sincere. "I'm grateful Katie came along. She's been more help to me than she realizes."

I put my arm around Carla's shoulders and noticed the other girls watching her carefully. "You are making a big difference in that young girl's life, you know."

She sighed. "I hope so. Losing Dad a couple of years ago was hard enough. I can't imagine going through that kind of grief as a kid."

Alice took Carla's hand. "You know that old saying—whatever doesn't kill you makes you stronger."

Carla frowned. "Yeah. What a stupid system."

We all agreed. Each of us had experienced wrenching losses at some point in our lives. At this moment in time though, we were all happy. I hoped it would be a while before hardship would visit itself again upon one of us.

# DECEMBER TWENTIETH

Francie stopped in to visit me the next day around noon, bearing chicken salad croissants from *Chez Gwen*.

"How are we going to manage a girls' night, when you and Emily are always working at the Christmas shop? I know Mom relies on you, but come on. Important tradition here. Memories waiting to be made, Mel."

I sighed, wanting a night with my besties but hesitant to dump my work on others. "Tassia Campbell is a big help, and Emily's mom, Jennifer Kincaid said if we need her, she's there. Kinda hate to do that since she works all day at the consignment shop."

Francie nodded, chewing the delicious concoction in ecstasy, and finally swallowed. "Everybody works all day at something else. You need to hire retired people."

"Hmm. There's a thought."

So it was that Lillian called her friend Reba Markland. Like many retirees in Serendipity, Reba was busier than ever, yet willing to help when needed. She was Emily's grandmother, and she took it on herself to contact Emily's mother to see whether she'd like to help too. Emily phoned to let me know the arrangements.

"So you ladies are good to go," she concluded.

"Emily, we want you to come with us."

"Oh no. This night is for the four of you who have been friends all these years. I appreciate the invitation, Melissa, truly, but I'll gladly work in the shop and make sure the night goes smoothly there."

"But you've done so much—"

"Hey, we're family. Plus I love planning weddings. Now, take my advice. You girls go out and have a big time. You all deserve the memories you'll make."

She sounded wiser than her years, but that was our Emily. When I hired her as a babysitter for Matthew, she was in her mid-twenties, but I thought she wasn't long out of high school. The car wreck that left a still-visible scar along her right jawline had started a series of changes in Emily. She looked her age now, but she spoke and behaved with wisdom and grace. I was fortunate to have her friendship, and the Standishes were thrilled David had made her part of their family.

I called Francie's cell to let her know.

"Sorry to ruin the surprise, but I heard already. Emily was here at Mom's when she called you. If you hurry, maybe you can be the first to tell Alice and Carla though."

"Think about what you want to do. I close the office at five."

"Honey, this is your party. What do you want to do?"

What indeed?

Matthew and one of his buddies at school had been begging for a sleepover, and the little boy's mother agreed tonight would work. She hoped the distraction of having an overnight guest would get her son's attention off a recent schoolyard debate of whether Santa was real. I think we both knew that wouldn't happen. Our boys were growing up quickly.

I was relatively certain I had provided a good foundation for Matthew to become a fine adult. Having Jim as his father full-time could only assist in that. I smiled, picturing the two of them together. Jim was a wonderful daddy, and the physical resemblance between the two was more apparent all the time. If I hadn't bought the old Osborne house and moved back to Serendipity, we might never have made the discoveries that came to light during that first Christmas season when Matthew was four years old.

The Osborne place. It was home now to Matthew and me. Jim and I had never come to a consensus about where the three of us would live after the wedding. Every time I brought up the positive aspects of living in town, Jim countered with the upsides of life on the farm. We weren't making any headway on a decision. Or to be precise, we'd each made our decision and wouldn't allow ourselves to be swayed from it. But something had to give. One house had to be the one for our new little family. In a few days it would be good to know where to go home to from the honeymoon.

The honeymoon that hadn't been planned.

When Carla answered the phone, she sounded frazzled. "Oh honey, I don't know," she said after I told her about the girls' night. "I should work. I've got some unfinished projects."

"Including your gold dress."

"Right. That has to come last. But don't worry—I'll get it done."

"It's you I'm concerned about, Carla. Maybe taking an evening off would be good for you instead of making you feel further behind."

"Maybe," she said doubtfully.

"How about we kidnap you for just a few hours?"

"I don't want to miss time with you girls. You know that, right?"

\*\*\*

I closed my office and drove Matthew to his friend's house. He was excited about the sleepover, but the Standish in him was strong. "Do you think Miss Lillian will be okay without me there helping?"

"Sweetie, she'll be fine. She's training some new people tonight, and tomorrow when you're there, you can ask her how work went." That satisfied him, and he grabbed his backpack and hurried up to the porch when I pulled into the drive.

The next stop was at the rear of Carla's shop where Francie and Alice emerged from Alice's car. Francie tried the shop door, but it was locked. Alice called Carla's cell. In a moment, she unlocked the door and motioned us inside.

"Wow, Carla. You look rotten."

"Gee, thanks, Francie. So glad you stopped by."

"We're here to rescue you, sister. Tell us what needs to be done and what we can do to help."

A shadow of a smile crept onto Carla's face. She led us toward the workroom and leaned on the dress rack on which hung several colorful creations. "Believe it or not, I'm finally caught up. I'd have been lost without Katie. Me—the woman who never needed an assistant. It's nuts."

"So if you're caught up why do you look so bad?"

"Old age?"

I nudged her. "Give me a break. You're two years younger than I am." I looked into her eyes, and the other girls were concentrating on her too.

"Oh my word!" Francie exclaimed. "You're in love. Nothing can mess with a woman's face more than unrequited love. Am I right?"

Carla whirled away from us. "Ugh. No comment."

Francie almost danced with glee. "Oh, ladies, what a great night this is going to be. An evening of toasting Mel and roasting Carla. I wouldn't have missed it for the world."

Instead of making the drive to Louisville, which is the norm when anyone in Serendipity had something to celebrate, we had dinner in town. We walked down to the *Barbeque Basement*. As usual, it was lively and loud, and the food and drinks were awesome.

"This is where Jim and I had our first date," I shouted.

"Can't be. It didn't exist when we were in high school," Francie yelled across the table.

"No. I mean our first date after I came back." The old Jim and Mel, and their untimely breakup had sure faded, in my mind.

Since we'd had some drinks, just to be on the safe side, we walked the few blocks from the restaurant to my house. The cold wind nearly took our breath away and stepping into the big warm house was a relief. We threw our coats in a pile and flopped on the sectional sofa where we spent the rest of the evening reliving memories and plotting our futures. Poor Carla probably wished she'd stayed barricaded in her shop. We pestered her endlessly, trying to get her to tell us who had stolen her heart.

She held up an unsteady hand that held a glass of red wine and shook her head. "Absolutely not. Whether I've fallen for someone or not doesn't matter right now. The only thing that matters is Mel and Jim—and Matthew." And she made yet another toast to our happiness.

# DECEMBER TWENTY-FIRST

Jim and I talked on the phone every night without fail. It was something I counted on and looked forward to, and I hoped he did as well. Unfortunately, last night I'd been in the noisy *Barbeque Basement* with the girls when his call came in. All four of us had taken turns giggling to him about this being my last night out with the girls as a single woman. I know there was more said than that, but have no clear memory of exactly what. This morning when I made coffee for the girls who'd all spent the night, my head hurt and I felt bad about Jim. In fact I couldn't remember the last time he and I had had a pleasant conversation. So much stress this month. Was his trial going well? Had I even thought to ask?

Francie walked into the kitchen yawning and running a hand through her short blond hair. "Love the guest rooms, Mel. My bed was super comfortable."

"Same here," said Carla, whose dark, under-eye circles were slightly less pronounced.

Alice strolled in, grinning. "That was my first night sleeping in a bed shaped like a pickup truck. Please thank Matthew for me."

I poured four mugs of coffee, and the girls took places around the tall table. "I'll be sure to do that."

Francie walked over to the glass doors that led out to the deck and pool. "I'm sure you'll miss this. The Osborne house has done its part in your life though, hasn't it? Got you back to Serendipity."

Alice and Carla looked at me.

"So you've decided to move to Jim's place?" Carla asked. "I wasn't sure who would win on that one."

I avoided their eyes, focused on watching the milk swirl into my coffee. "It isn't a matter of winning. And no, it hasn't been decided."

Francie turned toward us. "Oh. Well, if this is any help, I've heard you may have an interested buyer."

My breath caught. This was home to Matthew. My mind kept coming back to that simple fact.

Nodding, Francie joined us at the table again. "Yep. Tad, the oldest son of the Osbornes is taking early retirement, and he'd like to come back to town. To this house, if possible. You know the world revolves around Serendipity. Tad Osborne's company is a client of Brad's."

Alice touched my hand and wouldn't let me look away. "Sounds like it's meant to be. Living here has been cathartic for you, Mel. But wouldn't you agree a house is just a house? Isn't it love that makes it a home?"

And the love would be wherever Jim and Matthew and I were together. That would be our home.

Carla slid out of her chair and put her arm around my shoulders. "Mel, your family lived in a couple of houses when you were growing up, right? When you think of your childhood, what home comes to mind?"

I forced myself to relax for a moment, let myself be lost in the feelings of my childhood. Hot tears formed as the reality sank in. Reality I'd always known but recently had pushed away.

"The only home I knew as a kid was yours. The Standish house, the tree farm, was where I always had unconditional love."

Francie and Alice huddled around us. "It's there for you now too, Mel," Carla said. "For you and Matthew, if that's where you decide to live. We can paint trucks on the walls of his new room, you know. Or do a wall in chalkboard paint and let him draw his own."

An image of Matthew drawing on his walls, with permission, sprang to mind and made me smile. "I love that idea. He will too."

Francie wiped her own tears with a cloth napkin and offered it to the rest of us.

"This was supposed to be a fun girl time," I said, when I'd had my turn with the napkin.

Alice laughed, sniffing away the last of her tears. "It's been fun, but the kind of fun we needed, with just enough reality to make it a beautiful memory."

Returning to her place at the table, Carla raised her coffee mug in a salute. "Ladies, I'm afraid we're past the age of having a night like we just endured. We acted like teenagers."

Alice's brows rose after she took a big slug of coffee. "I disagree. We acted like women who enjoy spending time together."

"It's not as if we did anything awful," Francie said, massaging her temples. "Dinner and a few drinks, a few more drinks here, lots of catching up and making sure the bonds are still strong. Plus some good amateur psychology this morning with our coffee."

"Nobody did anything embarrassing last night," I pointed out. "I think it was good that Carla told us she has fallen for Jared Barnett. Now we're all on the same page and can be supportive."

Silence.

"I—what? I did not!" Carla frowned. "Did I?"

I reined in my smile a little bit. "Not until now, you didn't. Thanks, Carla. I think he's a good guy."

Her face turned crimson. "You tricked me, Mel."

"Of course. How else would we learn the truth? You wouldn't agree to our requests for a friendly game of 'Truth or Dare.'"

Francie and Alice excitedly started to talk over each other.

"Barnett? That jerk?"

"What do you mean he's a good guy?"

"Do you have any history on him?"

"Where's he from, originally?"

"Carla can't have fallen for a man with two kids. She doesn't even like kids."

Carla stood. "Of course, I like kids. And okay, I like Jared Barnett. But he's a widower and still grieving. A relationship with him would be way complicated, and to be honest, I'm not sure I'm up for it." She drained the rest of her coffee and set the mug down a little too hard. The sound reverberated around the room and through my aching head. "Besides, I don't think he's interested." Her eyes turned damp. She escaped from the kitchen, retrieved her coat, and slammed the front door before any of us could form a reply.

After a moment, Alice looked at us with unbelieving eyes. "A heterosexual, Earthling male not interested in Carla Standish? Is that even possible?"

# DECEMBER TWENTY-SECOND

Early in the day I received a text from Jim saying the trial was over. That was it—no elaboration or statement of the verdict. I texted Alice to be sure our late night hadn't caused her any difficulty with work.

*Nope. I'm good! Still reeling about Carla. ;)* was her reply.

That night Jim called at our usual time. "Hey, Mel. How are you? It seems forever since I've seen you."

"I know... I thought you might be at the farm tonight."

"David said he had it covered. Evidently, that Barnett guy is helping too. He's either not the jerk I thought or else up to no good. But David says he knows which side of a handsaw to use and is good with the customers. I guess he can't do any harm selling trees."

"He's not a bad guy, Jim."

"So you've said."

I wouldn't dare tell him how Carla felt about Jared. That was for her to do eventually, if anything came of it. I sincerely hoped it would. Carla deserved whatever happiness life offered because she was always creating happiness for others.

"You're sure about what you said last night—selling your house in town and moving into the cabin?" His voice was cautious.

"Yes, absolutely. The more I've thought of it, the more certain I am. Would you like to tell Matthew with me?"

He expelled a big, happy sigh. "Thanks, Mel. We're more of a family with each step."

"Yes," I whispered. "I'm so grateful for that."

After a moment, Jim cleared his throat. "I've been thinking."

I wasn't sure of the tone of his voice. "For some reason that sounds ominous."

He chuckled. "I hope not. I've made reservations for the honeymoon. Should I have cleared it with you? I thought you might enjoy having one thing off your plate and a surprise to boot. I think you'll enjoy it."

It was our honeymoon—the first time Jim and I would be together as husband and wife. Of course, I would enjoy it. But I'd seen the weather forecasts and wondered about travel.

"Flying? A lot of driving? They're predicting snow."

"I didn't book any flights, so you can wear lace-up shoes if you want without worrying about suddenly having to take them off. Let's see...what else can I say without tipping you off? Some driving. We should make it okay unless there's a blizzard."

Unfortunately, that was one of the words being used by some of the more experienced meteorologists.

"And the other part of my assignment—I've made arrangements for Matthew to stay with David and Emily for the weekdays and Mom for the weekend."

"Thanks for taking care of all that, Jim. You're right that it's a relief. I'll be glad to let our destination stay a surprise as long as it doesn't require me taking a different type of wardrobe than I'd normally pack."

"Mel, I don't think you'll need much wardrobe at all. I hope to stay in a lot. Maybe call room service occasionally if we need nourishment."

"Mmm. I get the picture. Sounds perfect, Jim. I can hardly wait."

"That's what I wanted to hear." He paused so long I wondered if the call had been dropped. "Mel, this has been the craziest month, and I know I've been a bear part of the time."

"Yes you have. Luckily, I know in reality you're a teddy bear."

"Do not spread that around. My successful law practice relies on people being fooled by my surly exterior."

I laughed. "I seriously doubt that. Everybody in Serendipity knows you're a good guy."

"Oh well. So much for a tough reputation. Tell me what's new with our wedding plans. Should I be doing something I'm not?"

It sounded wonderful to hear him say "our wedding plans." I hesitated to voice the one-word question: "Tuxedos?"

"They're ordered. David nudged me, not gently either. Actually, I think I got a call that they're here, so I need to drop by and pick them up tomorrow."

I moved my mouth away from the phone to sigh in relief. "That's great. Matthew's may be with them. How many groomsmen did you decide on?"

"Tuxedoes for me, David, and Matthew. I think that's about all the manly good looks the crowd will be able to take, don't you? Okay. Next order of business."

"We agreed those would be your only tasks, didn't we?"

"Hey, suddenly I'm available and agreeable at the same time. Don't squander an opportunity."

I pictured his face, the corners of his eyes crinkling as he made his jokes, his kissable mouth smiling as he enjoyed a relaxed conversation after some difficult days. It crossed my mind to bring up the topic of some tiny wedding details, but I didn't want to spoil this lovely conversation for both of us.

"Hmm. I don't want to wear you out, Jim. I want you nice and fresh for the wedding day…and honeymoon. So as long as you pick up those tuxes and show up tomorrow for the rehearsal, we're good."

"You've got it, Mel. I love you so much."

"I love you too, Jim."

I always had and always would, no matter what came our way.

# DECEMBER TWENTY-THIRD

Reverend Bobby had agreed to do the rehearsal at eleven in the morning two days before the wedding. Emily reported when she set it up with him that he didn't seem to mind the day as much as he minded the hour, so she promised him lunch. Reverend Bobby loves to eat. I had forgotten to schedule the traditional rehearsal dinner, but she bailed me out by securing a reservation for the back room at *Chez Gwendolyn*.

"I can't believe I'm getting so forgetful." I said nervously when she told me about the *Chez Gwen* luncheon.

She took me by the upper arms and looked into my eyes. "It's to be expected, Melissa. It'll be okay, I promise."

Another black mark on my permanent record—I had forgotten to choose any music too. I was relatively sure no one would ever ask me to help plan a wedding.

"No music? No problem," Rev. Bobby said reassuringly, watching me wring my hands. "I have lots of wedding music we can use before, during, and after. I must say I'm thankful you didn't opt for live musicians. That's sometimes a challenge. I've seen it all, believe me." He put a hand on my shoulder. "Melissa, see the young man in the choir loft? That's Alex who runs the sound system. He's terrific—he'll cue up the CDs just right. It'll be fine. Please stop worrying."

I hadn't realized my worrying was so apparent. For the last couple of nights I had slept very little and got up each morning with a headache from all the concerns circling in my brain through the night. Nothing useful though, like a rehearsal meal or hiring a musician. I forced a smile. "Okay. I'll try."

The rehearsal was interesting. I thought it would be very simple because we didn't want to do anything out of the ordinary with the service. Having the event on Christmas Day was unusual enough without including a sand ceremony, or writing our own vows, or one of us singing to the other.

Something about the lack of music and Jim having two attendants to my three made me feel off kilter during and after the rehearsal. I sat at the *Chez Gwen* table, clutching Jim's hand on one side and Matthew's on the other.

At some point, my son tried to squirm out of my grip. "Mommy, you're squeezing."

"Oh. Oh, I'm sorry Matthew." I released his hand and kissed his forehead. "I have a lot on my mind."

"Mr. Jim says you have a head full of wedding. Does it hurt?"

I looked at Jim who was smiling slightly, pretending not to be listening to us. "It does hurt, but just a little. And it'll be all better when the wedding is done."

Matthew shook his head. "I think you worry about it too much, Mommy. You and Mr. Jim could just get married right now, and then your head would stop hurting. Right?" He pointed down at the other end of the table where the minister was sitting. "Reverend Bobby could say the words and marry you."

"Oh golly, we don't want to do that, sweetie. We have lots of plans, and Miss Carla has made my pretty dress, and she and Miss Francie and Miss Alice have special dresses to wear too. And you and Mr. David and Mr. Jim get to wear fancy suits. We're going to make it a special day."

Matthew frowned. "Sometimes girls are hard to understand."

Jim and David roared with laughter. I looked up and realized everyone at the table had been listening to our little conversation. Well, at least Lillian and the girls were in my corner. We knew the memories of our wedding would be more special because of our effort to make them that way. I looked again at Lillian who had related the story of her wedding to Harry. Well, okay, at least Francie and Carla and Alice and I understood. And Emily, who was taking better care of me through all this than I deserved.

I leaned back in my chair and wished alcohol was one of the options at *Chez Gwendolyn*.

# DECEMBER TWENTY-FOURTH

Southern Indiana isn't the white Christmas capital of the world, by any means. So as more of the forecasters began to predict "measurable accumulation," excitement rose. When the phrase "winter storm watch" showed up on the TV and smart phone screens, there was another uptick of energy.

Snow began to fall and the tree farm was busier than usual, with people coming to browse the Christmas shop even though they'd already been to the farm earlier in the season to buy their tree. I made a run to the grocery for Lillian so she could restock the bags of wassail mix which were scooped off the shelves as fast as she could make it. There wasn't time to bake more cookies, but they'd have sold too.

"This is what Christmas should be. What it should look like, smell like, and taste like," one man had said. He and his wife and kids had stopped in for mugs of hot cocoa after a walk among the pines just because it was so peaceful.

His wife giggled, wiping snow off her daughter's dark curls. "I feel just like a kid hoping for a snow day from school. We don't have to travel this year for Christmas. We had a big gathering at Thanksgiving, and for Christmas, we're staying home. So let the blizzard come."

My stomach began to churn.

Carla put her arm through mine. She and I had both closed our businesses for Christmas Eve so the non-family help didn't have to work. "Mel, don't worry. It'll be fine."

"I hope you're right, Carla. It seems like everything possible is going wrong with our wedding plans."

"You're being negative, honey. That's not like you. Everything important is going totally right. You've reunited with the man you love, and you're surrounded by family and friends who couldn't possibly be happier for you. A little snow—even a lot of snow—can't ruin your day. It simply can't."

"I know you're right, Carla. It's just I have this picture in my head of how I want it all to look. Emily has helped so much, and you—wow. Without you, we wouldn't have those beautiful gowns." Her expression changed almost imperceptibly, and I noticed the strain she was trying to hide. "Did you get yours finished, Carla? I know you've been swamped this month."

"It's almost done. I only have maybe an hour of work to do on it, and I brought it home so I can finish up tonight. Brought all of them. This way, tomorrow will be easier—I won't have to make a trip to the shop before we head to the church." She smiled. "Everything will fall together."

Mostly, what fell was snow. By midafternoon, casual observers had stopped arriving to buy things from the shop and stroll through the trees in the quiet, deepening snow. I was relieved that Brad and Joseph had chosen to arrive yesterday. On an entirely different level, I was glad my parents and siblings in the central part of the state had opted not to attend the wedding even before the first prediction of snow had been made. Our only guests were local people, and I told myself repeatedly that it was highly unlikely for us to get enough snow that we couldn't all make it to the church tomorrow afternoon for the wedding. Seriously, what were the chances?

As the snow swirled around the Christmas shop, Lillian, Carla, Francie, Emily, Matthew and I chatted and drank cocoa or wassail, straightened the few remaining products on the shelves, expecting we'd seen all our customers for the season. There'd been a long lull when the door was flung open and a cold blast of air rushed in, carrying the Barnett family with it.

"Wow. This is awesome!" Miles exclaimed, pulling down his snow-encrusted hood. Matthew was around the counter in an instant.

"Hey, Miles!"

"Hey, Matthew! Dad and me are gonna build a snow fort. You wanna help?"

"Wow, yeah." He turned to me, his eyes glowing. "Okay, Mom?"

Jared looked sheepish. "Sorry to spring it on you, Melissa. The plan sort of evolved as we trudged over here. Originally, we were just out to get fresh air and maybe some cocoa."

"No, that's fine. It's a great idea." Matthew had been cooped up in this shop for enough hours this season and deserved a treat.

"That cabin is getting smaller all the time," Katie said through chattering teeth.

"I'll bet," Carla agreed. "You want to stay in here with us, Katie, or are you in a snow fort kind of mood?"

The girl's relief showed in her face and posture. "I'd like to stay here, if that's okay."

Lillian clapped her hands. "Well, isn't that nice. Cocoa?"

They all opted for cocoa before Jared and the boys bundled up again to go out.

Lillian started clearing away the mugs. "My sons always loved building snow forts. I wonder if they'll come and help you. I can walk over and ask...."

Jim and David had been barricaded in Lillian's kitchen with Brad and Joseph since the most recent tree purchaser had left a couple of hours ago. Lillian's dog Daisy was in there too. I doubted there'd be any food left in the house when they were done.

"Mom. Absolutely not," said Carla.

Lillian put her hands on her hips. "Why Carla. What a tone."

"I'm sorry, Mom. But after all the things that have gone wrong in the last few weeks, we sure don't need you getting out in this snow and falling on the way to ask the boys if they want to help build a fort."

Yeah. This was the same Carla who had chided me so recently about having a negative attitude.

Lillian bristled—something I didn't remember seeing before. "I've walked in more snow in my time than you have, my dear. And I am not ancient by any means."

"I didn't say you were, Mom. I'm just—"

Dean and Alice pulled into the parking area in his four-wheel-drive pickup. They hurried through the snow and onto Lillian's porch. "Go on in. The door's open," Lillian yelled from the entry of the Christmas shop, and they waved and did just that. She turned to me. "I invited them to spend the night, just in case. I feel sorry taking them from Christmas Eve with Tassia and Jack, but they all agreed this might be best."

I swallowed. "Just in case?"

Lillian nodded. "Everything will work out, Melissa."

For some reason, the more often I heard that, the less I believed it.

Due to the miracle of cell phones, nobody had to walk over to the house and propose the snow fort idea. A few minutes later, Alice made her way over to join us, and Jim,

David, Brad, Joseph, and Dean piled out of the house and met Jared and the boys. Brad and Joseph looked as enthusiastic as any of them, suited up in their borrowed work jackets, tall boots, and gloves from the mudroom that was Lillian's back entryway. The group disappeared behind the shed.

Alice laughed as she hung up her coat. "I swear, boys never really grow up, do they? Jim immediately got all huffy about Barnett taking Matthew out to build a snow fort. 'I'll show him how it's done,' he said."

Lillian nodded, setting a mug on the counter for Alice. "The boys always built them behind the house, near the shed where the buildings and that line of trees create a wind break."

"This can be Jim's guy time since he opted against a stag party," I said.

Francie laughed. "I don't think he would have invited Barnett to a stag party."

Carla cleared her throat and tipped her head toward Katie.

"Oops. Sorry Katie. Just talking men. They're so competitive, aren't they?"

The girl nodded thoughtfully. "Those men don't like my dad?"

"That's not quite it, honey," Lillian put her arm around Katie's shoulders. "They don't dislike him. They just don't know him well enough yet."

"This is perfect," Francie said. "An hour or two of male preening and bonding, followed by more preening and bonding over lots of hot cocoa and coffee. They'll remember it the rest of their lives."

I thought Francie was probably right. Although Jim said he didn't trust Jared, I knew the man's offer to include Matthew in the snowy endeavor would help melt Jim's hardened heart, even if Jim felt compelled to be competitive in the process.

Alice sipped her wassail. "Jim said he still had the wooden block forms in the shed from when he and David used to build snow forts."

Emily cringed. "No doubt. They are such collectors."

Alice said, "Dean hasn't played in snow in years."

Francie shook her head. "My husband and son almost never have. Somebody should take pictures."

"Good idea," I agreed. But instead we sat and visited while the indoor/outdoor sound system played background Christmas music we'd all stopped hearing weeks ago.

I fell into a reverie of two years past, the first Christmas Eve Matthew and I had spent in Serendipity. That day had been lovely, holding so much promise. The evening had ended in a bit of magic that none of us would forget. Jim and I had taken our time building our relationship again, and I was certain we'd done the right thing in not rushing.

Two years ago. Much was the same, yet much had changed. We were fortunate to have family and friends, old and new, here to share this special time with Jim and me. Today was fun and special in its own way, and I tried to hold onto that and not look out the window at the increasing whiteness.

In spite of all the reassurances, part of me wondered if there even would be a wedding. The same part that whined in my ear that we could have gone to the judge's office weeks ago and avoided all this fuss.

# DECEMBER TWENTY-FIFTH ~ CHRISTMAS DAY

"Happy wedding, Mommy!" Matthew patted my face and snuggled up to me.

"Mmm. Good morning, sweetie. Merry Christmas to you."

"I'm glad you and Mr. Jim are getting married on Christmas. It's the very best day!" Matthew jumped out of bed and ran to the window. "Wow. Looky, Mommy! It snowed again!"

I groaned and got up, pulling on the flannel shirt Jim had loaned me for a bathrobe. I buttoned it over his T-shirt I'd used as a gown. When I joined Matthew at the window where he had pulled the curtain away, my heart sank.

"Uh-oh, Matthew. That looks like a lot of snow."

"Yes! I love snow. Don't you, Mommy?"

"Well, yes, mostly. But sometimes a lot of snow makes it hard to do things you planned to do. And it might not be safe to drive on the roads if it's very deep or if it's icy." I smoothed his hair and pulled him close. "We'll just have to see."

We joined Jim in the kitchen. "Merry Christmas," I said and kissed him when he handed me a cup of coffee. "Breakfast smells wonderful. Aren't you the fine host?"

"Merry Christmas. And about breakfast—don't get too used to it, Mel. I seldom cook, but this morning, I was in the mood."

"Maybe you should cook breakfast every Christmas morning. That would be a lovely tradition."

"I'm glad to shoot for it," he said as he swept Matthew into his arms. "Merry Christmas, pardner. I think Santa came while you were sleeping. I bet he left things at your mom's house too."

Matthew scrunched up his face when Jim gave him a whiskery kiss but kissed Jim back. Then he wiggled to get down.

"Santa will be so happy I only have one house next year. It's extra work for him if I have two." When he hit the floor, he was already running around the bar and to the living area where several gifts were under the tree. "We need to hurry and open these so we can do the wedding!"

Jim and I exchanged worried frowns as Matthew opened the first package.

I sipped the strong coffee. "What do you think about the roads?"

He shook his head. "We're under a state of emergency. Just guessing the sheriff might not consider a wedding an emergency. Plus, I really don't want to get the whole family out on the road and risk an accident. I know my driving, but you never know about the other guy's." He tucked a strand of my hair behind one ear. "I'm sorry, Mel. Looks like we have to postpone."

The rest of the gift opening passed in a blur. All the hopes for this day, recently and back when we'd dated in high school, ran through my head in a frenzied swirl.

Jim brought me another cup of coffee and pulled me into his embrace on the couch near the tree. With an effort, I found comfort in the beauty of the moment. "I know you're right about postponing, but I can't help being disappointed. It felt like the perfect day for us to get married." I looked out the big front window at the strengthening sunshine. "Honestly, it still feels perfect...except for the fact that we can't get to the church."

Matthew set down the brightly-colored truck he'd just opened. "What do you mean? Today is the wedding."

Jim knelt down in front of him. "Pardner, I have some hard news for you." He took Matthew's hand. "Because of all this snow, we can't go to town for the wedding today after all. It's not safe on the roads, and we don't want anybody to get hurt. Right?"

Matthew's eyes were riveted on Jim's. He nodded somberly then looked at me.

"It's okay," Matthew said, brightening. "We can have the wedding here. Mommy can wear her snow boots with her pretty dress. We can have it in the trees! Okay?"

I shook my head. "Sweetie, for a wedding you have to have a preacher to do the ceremony. Not sure how to explain it, but there's a rule—"

"Miles's daddy can do it. He has before."

"What?" Jim exclaimed.

"Miles's daddy did a wedding in a dolphin house. Miles said it was weird and cool. He could do your wedding in the trees too."

"Katie told me something about that," I said, faint hope beginning to stir. "It was a family wedding, and Jared obtained a license so he could perform it. I don't know specifics or even if he would be interested in helping us."

"Sure he would. Me and Miles are buddies, and his dad wants to fit into our town. I think they fit already, don't you?"

"Hmm." Jim looked at me. "That's an interesting idea."

"Yay!"

"We don't know for sure yet, son," Jim said quietly.

Matthew paused, maybe noticing Jim's use of the term "son," which I hadn't heard him do before. The little boy took Jim's hand and reached for mine. I took his hand and took Jim's too. Matthew's eyes were shining. "Can we ask?"

"Well, I have the license in my purse...." Where it had been ever since we got it. I'd been so frazzled, I was afraid I would lose it if I temporarily put it in a "safe" place.

I felt a smile break out on my face. "The way Reverend Bobby explained it, the law only requires the bride, groom, and officiant. I guess, actually, we could do that. Maybe go down to Lillian's and do the ceremony in her living room."

Matthew crossed his arms over his chest and shook his head. "In the trees, behind Miss Lillian's house. Those big ones that are close together. It's like a church in there."

Jim grinned. "Not only that, but there's the mother of all snow forts. A lot of the snow is off the grass because we used it to build the walls. We can't have the wedding in the fort, of course. We wouldn't all fit." Jim looked at Matthew. "We should have built a cathedral while we were at it."

Matthew nodded. "Our fort is amazing. The best one me and Miles ever did."

\*\*\*

Carla fishtailed up the hill in her Mustang to bring the dresses. David and Emily, and Jim, Matthew, and I managed the trek easily in four-wheel drives, and David and Emily picked up the Barnett family as they drove past the tiny cabin they were renting.

Carla, Francie, Alice, and I changed in Lillian's big master bedroom. The sun warmed the day to about thirty degrees, and thank goodness, the breeze was light.

Lillian tapped on the door and entered, her face flushed. "Don't you all look lovely!" She kissed each of us on the cheek. "Funniest thing, but I can't find my Bible this morning. Could be nerves, I suppose." She huffed out a big breath and held up a large black Bible. "I've got Harry's though. He'd be so pleased for it to be used at your wedding."

When we went out the back door wearing our snow boots and tea-length dresses, I suddenly realized this was indeed the perfect day and perfect setting for our ceremony. Emily had turned on the Christmas music on the shop's indoor/outdoor sound system. The sun's rays transformed the snow into a million glittering diamonds. The heavy satin of my dress kept me reasonably warm, and though my big, wool-lined, LL Bean boots might have looked a little out of place, they easily got me up the slight incline past the mother of all snow forts, as I followed Francie, Alice, and Carla to the dense grove of evergreens. Matthew had been right. The large trees provided a windbreak and a natural "cathedral" type setting. Lillian was there in her big winter coat and the beautiful red wool hat Carla had given her for Christmas. Grouped around her were Emily, Katie, and Miles.

Next to Jared stood Jim, looking more than ever like the man of my dreams. He was handsome in his tux, the pant legs tucked neatly into his barn boots. His eyes held the reality of how precious he considered the love we had rediscovered. Standing beside him, hand in gloved hand, was Matthew, wearing clothes from yesterday but with a new, hand-knit toboggan cap on his head—a tradition Lillian had started the first Christmas we were in Serendipity. The miniature tux I had rented for him was hanging neatly in his closet on Main Street. On Matthew's left was David, looking nearly as pleased for us as he had been at his own wedding to Emily.

When I reached them, Matthew took my hand too. The moment was perfect as only unplanned happy surprises can be. We were surrounded by family—longstanding and newfound. Our little group fit perfectly into the space between the snow-laden trees.

Jared pulled a paper out of his coat pocket and unfolded it, his hands shaking slightly in his nervousness. He cleared his throat. "I thought we could start by hearing the Love Chapter—1st Corinthians 13." He flipped pages to find it, and a small bit of yellowed paper fluttered out of the Bible to the snow. Jared waited as Jim scooped up the paper and glanced at it. When his face paled I wondered if it had been a family obituary cut out and filed for safe keeping. It seemed everyone was holding their breath in concern that one more thing had gone wrong with our special day.

But the color returned to Jim's face, and with it a smile of pure joy. He held the clipping so I could see too. Harry Standish had cut out and saved our photos from the newspaper's annual high school graduation section so long ago. "Singer, Melissa" and "Standish, James" side-by-side, and waiting in Harry's Bible for over twenty years.

I'm not sure exactly what Jared said in the ceremony, but I know that just as Jim and I kissed at the conclusion, Bing Crosby started to croon *I'll Be Home for Christmas* over the loudspeaker. And those of us who remembered Harry Standish knew he was with us too.

*The End...or is it The Beginning?*

# A NOTE FROM THE AUTHOR

Thank you for reading CHRISTMAS WEDDING. I hope you enjoyed your visit to Serendipity, Indiana. This is Book Three of the series, and there are more to come. In order to be up-to-date, please visit my website at **www.magdalenascott.com**, and sign up for my newsletter. There's always something special—just for subscribers—in the newsletter. I only send one when there is actually news, so don't worry about me flooding your inbox!

Also, if you liked this story and are willing to write a review at your favorite online bookseller, I'd be very appreciative. Reviews are so important to authors, and as you know, they are important to readers too. Thank you for considering it.

Serendipity, Indiana Series
Small Town Christmas – Book One
Emily's Dreams – Book Two
Christmas Wedding – Book Three

Future Serendipity Titles
The Blank Book
The Road Not Taken
The Ring
A Piece of Her Soul

You can email me, sign up for my newsletter, and connect me via social media by visiting my website:
**www.magdalenascott.com**

www.ingramcontent.com/pod-product-compliance
Lightning Source LLC
Chambersburg PA
CBHW070632130626
46555CB00006B/2532